Endsville

I struggled over onto my side and found myself face to face with something far worse than any of my wildest nightmares.

It was covered with glistening black hair still dripping from the stream. Vents along both sides of the creature's body opened in unison. Its many eyes glared right at me.

I was frozen in place, too terrified to move....

the Swampland trilogy

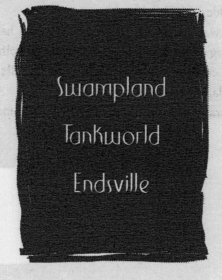

Swampland

Tankworld

Endsville

Endsville

S.R. Martin

POINT

SCHOLASTIC INC.
New York Toronto London Auckland Sydney
Mexico City New Delhi Hong Kong

No part of this publication may be reproduced in whole or in part, or stored in a retrieval system, or transmitted in any form or by any means, electronic, mechanical, photocopying, recording, or otherwise, without written permission of the publisher. For information regarding permission, write to Scholastic Australia Pty Limited, P. O. Box 579, Gosford 2250 Australia.

ISBN 0-439-10568-4

Copyright © 1997 by S.R. Martin.

All rights reserved. Published by Scholastic Inc., 555 Broadway, New York, NY 10012, by arrangement with Scholastic Australia Pty Limited. SCHOLASTIC and associated logos are trademarks and/or registered trademarks of Scholastic Inc.

12 11 10 9 8 7 6 5 4 3 2 1   0 1 2 3 4 5/0

Printed in the U.S.A.   01

First Scholastic Trade paperback printing, March 2000

Typeset in 12/15 Bembo.

Endsville

PART ONE

WHERE WE ARE

They tell me that from where we are you can see forever.

My people have carried me to the only vantage point for kilometres around, a loose jumble of massive granite boulders. There is a story about how the boulders are actually marbles left behind by the children of giants. It is a story, nothing more, but in my mind I can so easily picture those children towering out of the flat desert landscape, their faces alight with the joy of play; and the massive smashing and booming of the colliding granite mixed with the excited calls of the players. It brings a smile to my face.

I gather it is one of the recent myths, a jumbling of tales and legends from so many different cultures that no-one can tell where anything originated.

They have made me comfortable on this vantage point, arranging leather cushions stuffed with dried grasses, and facing me in the direction of the upcoming battle. There are defensive positions surrounding the base of the rocks. Generals flit in and about my senses like worker bees, while endless scouts arrive and depart, keeping us updated with the enemy's movements.

The only problem I have with being in a place like this is that I can neither stand nor see.

Not in any conventional sense. My legs went quite some years ago, and my eyes . . . well, my eyes went years ago, too, but not quite as far back as my legs.

I've compensated, though. Rather well. I use my arms to move short distances, or the others carry me if we're travelling far. And I have so many eyes now I sometimes wonder how I managed for all those years with just two.

People don't just see with their eyes, but with their minds as well, and the images they pass on to me are always tainted a little by who they are.

Rainbow, who is by far the youngest and most aggressive of my generals, sees everything as an opportunity for attack. He is always on at me for what he interprets as my indecision in acting upon his advice. Slap is older, having been with me from the very beginning, back when all the craziness started, and tends to see both the positive and negative of everything, weighing the good against the bad. While Anne, the only fully human general among them, is more of a wild card, coming up with suggestions which reflect our common heritage with those who wish to destroy us.

Three points of view.

Because of these different opinions, I am better able to deal with the enemy.

The Cyclists.

I have never seen a Cyclist with my own eyes—not the current variety. I remember what they used to look like. My brother, Marvin, rode a bike virtually everywhere. I even made him a trolley attachment for it so that he could tow his canoe down to the swamp near our parents' old house.

Rainbow has been in my ear since dawn, whispering about taking the initiative and attacking the Cyclists while they are unprepared, still trying to manoeuvre into a position of strength around us. But I have kept him on a close leash, not wanting his natural aggression to burst out suddenly and bring my grand plan to grief.

My grand plan. What a joke.

We are hopelessly outnumbered, underequipped and basically as close as you can get to the concept of extinction. I think I know how that last clutch of dodos must have felt as they shuffled nervously about in their nests, unable to fly, waiting for hunters to kill and eat them.

And that's exactly what the Cyclists intend to do with us, though what they're really after is the water.

The lake. Our home.

Without water, no-one can survive out here. And the lake where we live and breed is the only source of clean water for as far as any of us have ever travelled. How the Cyclists managed to journey so far from the remains of the cities I have no idea, but their mutations must hide many adaptations to life nowadays that I have little conception of.

I was blind before they first arrived, but I know what they look like. Anne's group once captured one alive and brought it back to the camp site by the lake.

It smelt like death, a sickening combination of decay and chemicals which hit you like a physical blow. When it opened its mouth to scream, fetid breath roared from its throat like a blast from a sewer, as if everything it had ever eaten had rotted inside it, so that all it spewed forth was airborne excrement.

I had them hold it down so that I could touch it and, as it kicked and struggled and vomited in rage and panic, I ran my hands from its head down to its feet. And though I'd had Cyclists described to me before, now that I was actually touching one and feeling its deformities, the horror was almost more than I could comprehend. For what I was touching, the thing bucking violently beneath my fingers, was what many of the human race had become.

Unbelievably, I was more closely related to it than I was to most of those that I lived with; and in its twisted, hideous shape were all the sins and mistakes of the generations before me.

It still had one of those plastic bike helmet things on its head, but it had been there so long it could not be removed. Skin had grown over the strap which held it to its neck, and it appeared that skin and hair had also grown out through the holes in the top of the helmet, so that the plastic had become like a second skull grown over the first. Mirrored glasses were also completely adhered across its eyes. After Rainbow smashed the lenses, the eyes were found to be a startling blue, like the eyes of newborn human children.

As my hands travelled down from the helmet, I found that its face was so wasted of flesh that it was like holding a bare skull in my hands (something I've done more than once in the last few years). There were no ears, just holes in the side of its head. Anne told me that all the Cyclists were like this. The only feature that was really prominent in its entire head was the mouth, a huge, slathering hole filled with hand-sharpened teeth. If Anne hadn't grabbed me as I explored its face, I would have lost the ends of several fingers.

From the head down, its neck, chest and arms were nothing more than skin clinging grimly to bones. And its skin felt strangely slippery, like it was silk or something similar, and I guessed that it must have been the remains of those brightly coloured shirts that bike riders used to wear, so old and unwashed that it, too, had become like another skin. When I asked the others, though, they were unable to confirm this. They said the thing was all brown and shiny and it was impossible to tell if it wore skin or clothing. I didn't want them to try pulling at anything in case they tore large sections of its flesh off.

As it was, everyone wanted to tear the damn creature to pieces anyway because of what the Cyclists had started doing to those members of our tribe they caught unprotected, but I needed to keep it alive so that I could understand what we were dealing with.

Around that time we had started finding the remains of small groups who travelled further away from the lake than the rest of us. We'd find the bodies of humans, but no sign of any Originals or Offspring. Occasionally, though, we'd come across a camp site deserted by the Cyclists, and there were always heaps of shattered bones lying about, many of them too large to have come from animals that lived in those parts. When these finds were put with the rumours that new human refugees brought with them, we began to piece together a picture. And that picture was ghastly.

Once my hands reached the Cyclist's waist, I recoiled in horror. It seemed that the creature was heavily padded with some incredibly hard material.

'What's it wearing?' I asked Anne.

'Nothing,' she replied. 'As far as I can tell, that's its body.'

Forcing myself to reach out and touch it again, I found that from the waist down the creature was hugely developed, with buttocks and thighs like those you used to see on Olympic speed skaters. The muscle development was simply awesome, as if its metabolism had decided to channel every skerrick of nutrition into developing those parts of its body which it used for transport. It was like two entirely different creatures grafted together at the waist: a hideous, malnourished skeleton for the top half, and a steroid-inflated athlete at the bottom.

'Are they all just like this?'

'Most of them,' Anne whispered. 'Though the children don't seem so bad. Maybe the changes become more pronounced after they start riding.'

'Children?'

I'd assumed creatures this deformed must also be sterile, but I was obviously wrong about that. It put an end to my hopes that the Cyclists would simply die out over time and that all we'd ever have to do was avoid them until there were too few to worry about.

'There aren't many children,' Anne continued, 'but enough. They are breeding, Zac. It's hard to tell from a distance because the females carry their babies on their fronts so they can feed them while they're riding. But there are children, there's no argument about that.'

This was another thing we'd discovered about the Cyclists: they never stopped riding unless they were about to camp for the night. And even then a great many of them never bothered to actually get off their bikes, simply leaning together in groups to eat and sleep. It was as if the bikes had become extensions of their bodies and to get off them was like cutting off an arm or leg.

Cyclists could walk, of course, and our scouts had watched them at their camp sites as they loped about in odd half-crouches, their bodies so used to riding they retained their posture even when walking. But it was obvious that they preferred not to be in contact with the ground for long, their world now almost entirely defined by two wheels.

In contrast to their bodies, the Cyclists' bikes are

immaculate, constantly oiled and cleaned and adapted. The old inflatable tyres have gone, replaced by tightly wound strips of material. But apart from that they are as perfect as the day they were made.

We didn't discover anything more from the captured Cyclist because it died later that night. Anne said that it looked as if it had simply given up on living because it had been separated from its bike, but I had my suspicions.

When I asked Rainbow if he knew anything about what happened, I could hear a definite nervousness in his reply, a tinge of guilt, but I was in no position to prove anything, so I simply let it ride. There was no point in confronting him about what I believed he had done as most of the tribe would have supported his actions.

Had my past history been any different, I could have ended up as a Cyclist. But to be one you need legs. And anyone whose legs fail them dies by the wayside or becomes food, depending on whether or not they consider you fully human. It's racism on a grand scale. The human race versus the others. The old takes on the new. Winner eats all.

By 'the others', I mean us.

'Us', should you care to look in a dictionary (if you can ever find one—books are something of a premium these days), is defined as 'I and other persons', which perfectly explains the make-up of our tribe. There's me, and then there are all the others I've had a hand in bringing together.

Naturally, there are pure-breed humans like Anne and myself, remnants of that seething culture which once infested the surface of this planet, survivors of war and pestilence of their own creation. Then there are the Originals, the group I guided through the very bowels of the earth for more years than I care to remember, whose parents' genes were spliced with those of fish in a laboratory, and whose escape from the American military makes up a large part of my past. Then there are the Offspring, our children, who came from the union of the two groups, and in whose hands lies the very future itself.

And we are at war for their future, but not because we choose this path. It has been forced upon us by the Cyclists, who devour everything in front of them like a wave of cannibalistic locusts.

I can still remember when you would see a cyclist in the street and not give him or her a passing thought. And even as far back as the end of the last century, when they had started to gather into packs for protection and aggressively took up half of the roadways in their meandering, they were still something which nobody feared.

My ruminations are interrupted by a sudden flurry of activity.

Scouts have arrived with the news that the Cyclists are moving. There has been some sort of activity off to the south-east, a direction I had least anticipated trouble to come from. It is to our rear and on the far side of the lake. For the Cyclists to attack from that direction would be suicide, as they would be out in the open for too long. But you never can tell what motivates the Cyclists. Their migrations have been relatively mindless, moving with the spontaneous decision of flocks of birds—until quite recently.

I can hear Slap screaming orders to his runners, as the lake and its surrounds are his responsibility. We have very few troops there, as neither Slap nor I thought it would be a problem. But that is also where our children are sheltering and, more than anything, it is our children we wish to protect.

'We have to regroup,' Rainbow says from quite close by. 'I'll take some of my people and wait under the surface until they attack. They won't know what hit them.'

'No,' I reply without having to think too much about his suggestion. 'Slap knows exactly what to do. I need you here, Rainbow. Anything that happens down near the lake has to be a distraction. They can't win down there and I think they know it. We'll be doing exactly what they want if we react too strongly to anything from that direction. They're trying to drag us away from here, can't you see that?'

'I can see a large cloud of dust heading towards the lake, Zac,' comes his surly reply. 'A *very* large cloud. Why don't you think we're already doing what they want? If we stay here and they attack the lake, we won't have anything to go back to. I hope you know what you're doing.'

This is something I can't be absolutely sure of, but there has always been something in the back of my mind that keeps telling me the lake will be fine. And I trust Slap completely, far more than Rainbow. If it wasn't for Slap I would never have made it through the tunnels under the Nullarbor, never have been capable of reaching the surface of the lake, and never have had a chance of surviving in the new world we discovered when we arrived. Slap has become as close to me as my long lost brother, and if he can't handle whatever happens down at the lake then no-one can.

Then Slap is beside me as well.

'I've got to go, Zac,' he says, his hand on my shoulder. 'I need to be there to direct things. Rainbow's right about the numbers, though. There are a lot more of them coming from that direction than we anticipated.'

'How many?' I ask.

'We can't tell yet, but they're kicking up a lot of dust.'

'Haven't the scouts got any idea? Surely they must have got close enough to see.' The information, scant though it is, is making me nervous.

'None of the ones we sent out in that direction came back,' he says quietly. 'We're just judging from the size of the dust cloud. I can handle it, though, no matter what they intend to throw at us. It just means that more of them will die there than we thought.'

I reach up and hold his hand in mine. 'Take care, brother. We'll have some great stories to tell when this is over.'

'Or we'll meet again in the water.' His lips gently touch my face and he is gone.

'They're coming this way, too,' someone shouts.

From the distance I hear a weird ululation, a cry which comes from many throats and sends chills running up and down my spine. It is the battle call of the Cyclists, a sound I've heard before over the years, but only ever given voice by small numbers of the creatures. Now it comes from many hundreds, and its effect is terrifying.

'Now we're for it,' I whisper.

'You can say that again,' chuckles Rainbow. 'But then so are they.' He's always been enthused by the thought of battle, something I have never developed a taste for. But then I've experienced it more often than he has, and I know just how desperate and ugly it really is. All Rainbow has ever done is engage in a skirmish or two and listen to the stories the Originals tell about our battles through the underground caves and tunnels as we made our way to the lake.

I suppose it is our fault that he is so eager to go off and die. But then we all may be dead soon, and through no fault of our own. All we've ever wanted to do is survive. Perhaps it is glorious to defend that desire?

I check the knife in my belt for reassurance. It is always there but I like to check anyway as it makes me feel more capable. As capable as a blind person without legs can be when faced with the prospect of death.

PART TWO

WHERE WE WERE

There was a time when things weren't as complicated in my life, a time when things were easier to understand, back when I was a teenager with a mother and father and younger brother. They're probably all dead now.

It began a little over fifteen years ago with something called love, I guess.

Marvin fell in love with Edie, the girl who moved in next door—and then everything turned to crap.

It was her twin sisters, Violet and Mauve, who were the real problem. They were the highly successful versions of their American parents' experiments into splicing human and fish genes, and, while Marvin was trying desperately to get Edie's attention, the twins were down at the swamp feeding up on the neighbourhood pets and spawning.

To give them their due, the American scientists at least saw the value of the experiments, though what their motive for creating them was and why they were so hell-bent on getting them back is beyond me. Maybe they knew what would eventually happen to the world and saw the Originals as our only hope for the future.

Marvin and I set the swamp on fire, and in the following conflagration the twins—and probably

Marvin—died. Though Edie and I were horribly burned, she dragged me out for some reason. She said she also managed to rescue Marvin, but I've always had my suspicions about that. I think she only told me that so that I wouldn't feel so bad and to ensure I remained loyal to her. This was unnecessary, as I'd already fallen for her in the same way that Marvin had. I mean, who else would I fall for? Who else could she fall for? The two of us were so disfigured by the fire, our skins slick and shiny with scar tissue, that even to look at us was hard.

Edie and I ended up out on the Nullarbor at a place called Tankworld. It seemed ordinary enough—a property where they sold water tanks and the like to the surrounding farms—but was the base for a group of scum who lived off the proceeds of robbing stranded tourists. There was a group of feral children living in a cave under the tanks on the property. They had managed to get away from the family that ran the place and were planning to escape by following an underground stream down to the ocean.

I was delirious through most of this. My legs, though useless anyway, had been broken in a fall and the resulting infection had sent me a little mad. While Edie and the children were raiding the farm for what they needed for the escape, I severed my legs completely with an old hacksaw. It freaked everyone out a bit, but it was the best thing to do. It cured the infection and made it much easier for me to move around.

Anyway, while the children finally made their escape downstream from the cave, Edie went back to the surface to collapse the tunnels because the American secret service was closing in on us.

Edie—it pains me even now to remember her—made the ultimate sacrifice so that I could escape with her nieces and nephews; in those days the Originals were little more than tadpoles with human arms and legs. Edie and I used to call them wrigglers.

When Edie didn't return, the wrigglers and I entered the stream, going in the opposite direction to the escaping children. The wrigglers are freshwater creatures. To have escaped to the sea would have meant death.

So began a subterranean life, a life of darkness and fear, of pursuit and encounters with things that had little relevance to the life I had left behind. But also a life through which I became bound to the creatures in my care, as our balance of debt steadily altered until it was me who felt I owed them a life rather than the other way around.

Year blended into year, until I was so used to twilight, the sun became only a memory. A dangerous one, in my case.

And all the while the human race was busily trying to wipe itself off the face of the earth, committing such sins in the name of progress that Nature finally revolted against them, turning food into slow poisons which sent those who ate it mad, and mutating viruses until the very act of procreation itself became like suicide. And then there were the man-made biological plagues released in times of war, the chemicals which seeped into the waterways and a million other crimes too hideous to mention.

It was inevitable, I guess, and I often speculate on where I would be had I not been hidden while all the trauma came to a head. Dead, most probably, like the majority. Like my family. Or carried along as some deformed mascot for the Cyclists, the cockroaches of humanity.

I tell you all this now in case I have no time to do it

later. There may not be a later, and it is essential to leave some record of our history, to show that we lived lives with some sense of purpose and dignity, and that, if we are wiped off the face of the earth by the Cyclists, someone somewhere will know that we tried to make a proper go of it.

The underworld is a place of caves and tunnels, of streams and lakes, darkness and luminescence.

We descended into it, and from it we have arisen.

3

There are things down there that defy imagination, that are the end result of the abuses we enact on the land above; things that have mutated and adapted to an existence we surface dwellers have no conception of.

It was not my decision to leave Edie behind in the desert, it was hers. I had no choice, you have to understand that. And isn't that what life's really all about, making choices you'd rather not have to make?

Try and imagine my predicament.

Apart from the wrigglers, I was alone, and the only information I was getting was the sound of gunshots and helicopters filtering down through the earth. The wrigglers knew something was happening, and they were agitated, crawling all over me, leaping in and out of the stream, waving their tiny arms and legs about in a frantic effort to communicate their fear.

We'd already waited half an hour longer than we'd promised, and I knew if it had been Edie instead of me she'd have taken the plunge already. Mind you, she was a lot better equipped to go swimming through water-filled tunnels than I was. All I had was an old scuba tank (with no idea of how much air it contained), a badly perished wetsuit and diving mask, and a waterproof torch that worked only when it felt like it.

Finally, with the sound of the helicopters still chugging in the distance and the flames from the torches in the cave guttering out one by one, I pulled the tank onto my back, gathered the agitated wrigglers into one group and slipped into the freezing water.

My last image of the cave that had sheltered us was the sight of my two sawn-off legs standing upright against the wall, looking like props left behind by a circus clown.

As the water closed over my head, blocking out all sound except its own rush in my ears, I felt as if I was leaving the life that I knew behind me forever.

(This, I must add, was not a new sensation for me. I'd already experienced it at least twice before. The first time was when I lost the use of my legs in a car accident, the second when I left my family behind to go with Edie, though I didn't have a lot of choice on that occasion.)

It was eerie in the tunnel, like some psychedelic nightmare, all colour and shape, image blending with image in a kaleidoscope of confusion.

Holding the torch in one hand I pulled myself along with the other, working against the flow of water, breathing as shallowly as possible to conserve my unreliable source of air. The wrigglers surged ahead in the beam of light, swimming with arms, legs and tails—a talent I would have given my left leg to emulate, had I not given it already.

The tunnel seemed to be formed from a lot of soft curves which all flowed into each other. Speckled throughout were flecks of different colours, mineral deposits of some kind. They picked up the light, glittering and flashing like hints of partially buried treasure, often so bright I'd think for a moment that someone else was down there with us. Occasionally I'd see movement ahead, but it only ever turned out to be small rocks being forced along by the current, which was gentle but constant. I guess it was these, combined with the movement of the water, that made the surrounding walls so smooth.

We were searching for another cave, somewhere we could shelter for a while without the threat of invasion from above, and I hoped that my supply of air would hold out until we did. The underground waterways, according to Josh (the oldest of the group of children that had escaped in the other direction), were a system of tunnels and caves, some of them completely submerged, others with sections that were quite dry, like the one we'd left behind. How far we'd have to go before we found one I had no idea, but it was essential that we did fairly quickly as I didn't relish the idea of spending my last days as a permanent fixture in an underground tunnel.

By way of contrast to my spluttering, struggling self, the wrigglers were surging ahead with unreserved enthusiasm, often disappearing completely from the steadily weakening beam of my torch. The first time they did this I felt a great bubble of panic swell up in my chest at the thought of being deserted in that isolated place, so totally alone that no-one would ever know what had happened to me. But they always came back, their little mudskipper shapes suddenly appearing ahead of me, then swirling all around my head like bait fish at the end of a jetty.

I was inordinately grateful to them for not leaving me, when, in fact, it should have been the other way around, but I wasn't in the position to think rationally at the time. They were all I had, and I'm sure that, had they left me, I would have completely lost my senses, spitting out my air supply so that I could drown quickly and not have to worry any more.

After what seemed like hours of moving along—but could only have been minutes—I had to take a rest, the strain in the arm I was using to drag myself along becoming so bad it would shudder violently every time I took a grip on the tunnel floor. I managed to wedge myself sideways, allowing the stumps of my legs to take most of the pressure while I held myself in place with my shoulders. The tunnel was not very wide where I rested, so the current was a little stronger than usual. It was, however, the only place I could stop without fear of being dragged back the way I had come.

I was completely exhausted and found myself almost drifting off to sleep. There was no sign of the wrigglers. They were still swimming strongly upstream the last time I saw them, but I imagined they'd return when they realised I was no longer bringing up the rear. At least, I hoped they would.

The air I was breathing had a nasty taste to it, old and musty, like it was second-hand. It seemed to stick in my throat and lungs, leaving a residue that felt like a thin coating of slime. Not knowing much about scuba, I hoped it was because the air had been in the tank for so long. The other option was that I was rebreathing my own used air, which would eventually prove fatal. Then I realised that every time I breathed out bubbles would escape, which meant that I couldn't be pushing air back into the tank.

Thankful for the fact that I could still reason things out, I relaxed a bit, switching off the torch to conserve the battery—which was when my air supply ran out altogether.

It happened so suddenly it was like receiving an unexpected punch to the abdomen. Without any warning, there simply wasn't anything more to breathe. It was as if I was trying to suck air from a lump of granite.

There was one thing to be grateful for, however, and that was the fact that it happened halfway through an intake of breath, so there was something in my lungs to go on with. Not that that occurred to me at the time. All I felt was a sudden, thrashing panic which needed every skerrick of mental discipline I had to overcome.

My body simply wished to claw its way through the roof of the tunnel to open skies where there was more air than I could ever possibly hope to breathe. The rational part of me knew that, unless I was extremely lucky and very calm, I was going to die.

I knew that I would never make it back the way I'd come on the half-a-lungful of air I had, so the only option left was to keep going forward. I eased the now useless tank off my back.

Switching the torch back on, I found the wrigglers had returned and were hovering in a small cloud just in front of my face mask. As soon as they saw the light, they moved off up the tunnel, always keeping within range of the torch beam.

I soon began seeing stars. They were large, bright ones, and they'd come swooping in from the extremities of my vision like out-of-control comets, tails all a-blaze, and explode smack bang in the centre of my head. I was beginning to become quite fixated on them, trying to guess which colour the next one would be, when the wrigglers started to throw themselves against the face of my mask.

We'd been moving upstream for perhaps a minute, maybe longer, and I'd just about given up hope of getting anywhere. Any air that remained in my lungs was so devoid of oxygen that it probably couldn't have been classed as air any longer.

For a few seconds all I could do was look into the wrigglers' faces, which I realised were now quite human. You could see every tiny detail: eyes, noses, mouths and, more revealing, expressions. They seemed to be trying to tell me something, and it took some time to realise what it was.

Then a series of sharp pains in the hand I was using to hold myself to the tunnel floor brought me back to my senses. The wrigglers were biting my fingers, which had frozen in a death grip to a lump of rock. I let go, flicking the wrigglers away, and suddenly bobbed up to the tunnel roof.

A strange sensation gripped me by the back of the neck and it took a second for it to register. It was air.

I was floating face down in a gap in the tunnel, the back of my head above the surface of the stream. All I had to do in order to breathe was turn over, which, in my weakened state, was something of a tall order.

Putting one hand above my head, I managed to slowly turn and, when my mouth found itself free of the water, it opened and a rush of ice-cold air filled my lungs.

It felt like someone had poured liquid fire into my chest and I was racked by a series of harsh, hacking coughs. I've never felt more glad of anything in my life.

I lay there sucking great lungfuls of air, feeling the wrigglers bumping against the side of my face at water level, tears bursting from my eyes.

Though I could breathe again, I was still a long way from being out of danger. The gap I found myself in was no more than a few centimetres high, so the only part of me that was out of the stream was my face and, every time the water in the stream surged a little, it would come up and cover my eyes and mouth again, causing a fresh bout of coughing and spluttering.

Now that I was part-way out of danger, though, I wasn't going to give up.

I brought my hands up and started to drag my tired body along the tunnel and, as I went, I found myself with more room. It wasn't a lot to begin with, just a centimetre or so for every few metres of progress, but the gap was definitely getting bigger.

Eventually, the entire front of my body was free of the water, buoyed up by the wetsuit. I could now shine the torch behind my head, illuminating the tunnel, which continued to widen the further it went. Eventually I had to start dragging myself along the side wall.

The cave, when it suddenly opened up in front of me, was so large it defied the reaches of my depleted torch. I could see neither the roof nor the far end, but I did make out the wide shelf along one side. It jutted out about twenty or so centimetres above the level of the stream. When I reached it I had to hang there for quite some time before I could summon the strength to haul myself out of the water.

The last things I remembered were the feel of dry, powdery sand under the side of my face and my thumb, almost as if it were functioning by itself, slowly managing to push the switch of the torch to OFF.

I have no idea how long I slept after I first made it to safety in the cave. It could have been minutes or hours or even days; my understanding of time and its passing was never the same after I entered the tunnel. Darkness distorts things so that they have no relevance to what you knew in daylight.

Once I opened my eyes, however, I knew for a fact that I was dead.

There are creatures in this world that never see daylight, that are born and live their entire lives without ever approaching what we call the surface of the planet. A lot of them are blind and make their way through touch and smell and vibration. Others, though, have eyes. Why, you may ask, do creatures have eyes when they live in complete darkness? How can they see? These are good questions, and the answers were as plain as the nose on my face when I opened my eyes in that underground cavern.

Though, to begin with, I had no idea of what it was that I was seeing.

Having fallen asleep in complete darkness, I awoke to light, but unlike any I had ever seen before. I had the uncomfortable sensation that I had arrived in heaven, and what was bothering me was the thought that a mistake had been made, that I'd arrived in the wrong place, and any second a large white creature with wings was going to pop up, apologise for the error and send me in the other direction. I had, after all, been a thief and a brawler, had some pretty raunchy thoughts about Edie and done enough other nasty stuff to have a permanent black mark against my name.

But I wasn't in heaven and I wasn't in the other place either.

All around there was an ethereal glow, a disturbing ghostliness every way I looked. I eased myself upright, the feel of the rock wall behind me confirming the fact that I was still alive, still trapped within the real-life nightmare I had escaped through sleep.

It was now possible to see the extent of the cavern which stretched away for at least a hundred metres from the shelf that had been my salvation. The roof was a cluster of stalactites which, as one moved further into the cave, met with stalagmites growing from the floor. Scattered amongst the icicle-like growths were weird clusters of fungus, and it appeared as if the glow I was seeing came from these.

'Neon mushrooms,' I muttered to myself, 'just what I need. Add toast and some black pepper and I'll have a breakfast that lights its way through my intestines. Not to mention what it'll do in a toilet bowl!'

I looked about for the wrigglers but they were nowhere to be seen, though I could make out the imprints of their tiny feet all around where I'd been lying on the sand shelf.

'Hello?' I called, and my voice echoed through the cave, coming back several times, as if steadily smaller versions of myself were hiding in out-of-the-way places.

Apart from that, there was no reply. It felt as if I was now completely alone, that my charges had given me up for dead and gone on their merry way further along the waterway, which I could see disappearing into the rock wall at the far end of the cave.

That'd be right, I thought. I nearly get myself killed leading them out of danger and they go and desert me in a place where I've got no chance of escaping from myself. Nice. Very, very nice. I'm going to starve to death.

Sighing in resignation, I slowly made my way along the shelf, using my arms to swing my body in small arcs. The stumps of my legs had no sensation, even though they were still a way from being healed and, for once, I was glad of my handicap. My knuckles, on the other hand, hurt like hell from carrying the entire weight of my torso. It was a method of movement I would become quite accustomed to, but at that stage it was new to me and I hadn't adjusted to it.

(I must admit, though, that for the first time in years I was actually able to move about under my own steam, without the aid of a wheelchair or having to drag myself along the ground like a lizard. Had I known earlier that removing my legs would have made getting about easier, I might have given them the flick a long time ago.)

The shelf I'd first arrived on widened out the deeper I went into the cave and, as I travelled along it, I had to negotiate my way around the stalagmites, some of which were so high they joined the stalactites hanging from the roof. The cave itself had to be at least seven or eight metres high, so you'll have some idea of how impressive these structures looked. The stream by which I'd entered ran the entire length of the cave along one wall. The rest of the place was simply dry sand interspersed with rock icicles and clusters of glowing fungus, though on closer inspection I could see that there was more than one type of the latter.

I had the feeling that I was the first person ever to have set foot (or knuckles) in the place, and that made me feel very alone.

Moving through the strange structures all around me, it seemed as if I had arrived on the set of some science fiction film, somehow landed inside the crashed spacecraft in *Alien*. Any second, I expected one of the clusters of fungus to open up and some nasty looking creature with lots of legs to attach itself to my face and thrust an appendage down my throat.

I made a slow circuit of the entire cave, looking about in corners for wrigglers. They were nowhere to be found.

At one stage, I reached out and touched a clump of the fungus, and found that whatever was causing the glow came off in my hand. I wondered what would happen if I ate any of them, whether I too would start to glow in the dark like some cheap plastic novelty at the Royal Show.

Having explored my new environment, there wasn't a lot else for me to do. I'd pretty much done my dash. Sure, the wrigglers and I had escaped from the Americans and the possibility of capture, but where that now left me I had no idea.

I was trapped, for starters, unable to either move further along the system of underground waterways or return from the way I'd come. The wrigglers might be able to move around through the stream, but I'd be about as comfortable down there as a turkey at Christmas.

Propping myself against a large stalagmite, I spent some time experimenting with the flashlight, using up the final dregs of power by flicking it on and off and watching the changes that happened in the cave.

It was certainly unusual. When the flashlight was on, the cave returned to darkness and all you could see was what was caught in the weak yellow beam it threw out. However, if I switched it off, after a couple of minutes the glow from the fungus would start to illuminate the entire cave again, eventually building up to that strange, ethereal glow that had convinced me that I had passed on from one life to another. I knew that there must be some scientific explanation for it, but my mind was too overwhelmed to try and reason it out.

Finally, in a guttering flicker, the batteries gave out completely, and I sat there as the cave returned to its natural state of illumination.

I hurled the useless flashlight as far up the stream as I could.

As it hit the water, a strange disturbance occurred, as if something large just underneath the surface had raised itself up and twisted about, annoyed at the intrusion. Nothing actually broke through, but you could see clearly that something had moved up and then down again, because water gushed out of its natural bed and stained the dry sand.

There was a sound as well, like an underwater fart, which echoed as my voice had done earlier, repeating itself in smaller and smaller versions.

The hair on the back of my neck stood up and I shivered uncontrollably. I backed as far away from the stream as possible. Apart from the absent wrigglers, I'd been under the impression that I was alone in the cave, about as far from company of any kind as a human being could get. This was obviously not the case.

Something else was down there with me, and I really didn't feel like meeting it right at that second, not until I'd found something to protect myself with anyway.

I looked around for a weapon, but all that I could see was the perished diving mask that I'd used to get through the tunnel. Even the flashlight was gone, and I didn't fancy diving around in that section of the stream to retrieve it.

Shivering with fright, I put my back to the cave wall and sat waiting for whatever was going to emerge from the stream. I wondered what had happened to the wrigglers, but only briefly, my main concern at that moment being my own survival.

I guess I was pretty close to total madness at that stage. A song kept running about in my head, one of those annoying numbers that just seems to stick. Eventually I gave voice to it, 'Home, home on the range, where the deer and the antelope play . . .' That's all I could remember of the words, so I kept repeating them. And as the echoes of my voice joined me, it seemed as if I was no longer alone down there, that my miniatures were arranged around the walls of the cave singing rounds with me.

The words were strangely prophetic, I realise now. In the end, the cave (the entire cave system eventually) became our home for many years.

Only it wasn't a home *on* the range. In our case it was *under* it.

When I woke again, I toppled forward and landed face first in the sand, letting out a shout of alarm and struggling until I managed to right myself. I had no idea when I'd fallen asleep, but now that I was awake I was immediately on my guard, my eyes searching the far corners in case what had made that hideous sound had crept from the water and was sneaking up on me, using stalagmites as cover.

All was quiet, however, and after a few minutes of nervous peering I relaxed and started to wonder about the wrigglers. Though I'd seen what I took to be their footprints in the sand, I hadn't actually set eyes on them since I first arrived and their absence was making me nervous.

So much for gratitude, I thought.

There was something else nagging at me as well, and it took a few minutes before I realised it was hunger. It had been hours since I'd last eaten, if not days, and my stomach was making itself known in the worst possible way, snarling and growling over its neglect.

I cast a quick glance at the glowing fungus but didn't think I was quite that desperate yet. Mind you, at the rate my stomach was going, it wouldn't be long before I'd be forced to sample the local vegetation, poisonous or not.

Then the strangest thing happened. Suddenly, all along the edge of the stream, the surface of the water was broken by tiny figures which leapt up onto the bank. My mouth dropped open in surprise, because what emerged from the water were dozens of fish fingers equipped with arms and legs, which came scampering across the sand towards me.

I laughed delightedly, my whole body shaking in amusement until I lost my balance and toppled face forward into the sand again. My last thought was that I must be hallucinating, as fish fingers couldn't walk as far as I remembered, even the most expensive varieties. Mind you, the one that stood in front of me with its arms on its hips looked pretty damn real, and very appetising.

I was still giggling when darkness overwhelmed me.

A disgusting taste brought me back to consciousness as effectively as a bucket of cold water poured over my head.

My first reaction was to spit, as my mouth seemed to be half-filled with a combination of blood and fish, but hunger overwhelmed my natural response and I swallowed before I even knew what I was doing.

I gagged violently, but it stayed down.

As I lay on the sand, half-propped on my elbows, retching and moaning with tears streaming from my eyes, I felt a gentle touch on my cheek. Blinking away moisture, I finally focused on a figure standing next to my head. I was one of the wrigglers and it was looking at me with an expression of curiosity combined with concern.

It reached out and touched one of the tears running down my face, lifted it to its mouth and tasted, the wriggler's face registering disgust at the saltiness.

The wriggler made hand-to-mouth motions, then pointed back over my shoulder. I rolled over and sat up, discovering a crowd of wrigglers clustered around something next to the stream. They were milling around excitedly, boiling over each other to get at whatever it was.

Remembering the hallucination I'd had before fainting, I wondered what the wrigglers' reaction would be if they knew what I'd been thinking a short time ago.

I lurched towards the others, still tasting the foul concoction of blood and fish. I was fairly certain that my guide had placed whatever it was in my mouth, and had the uncomfortable feeling I was just about to discover what it had been. What my stomach's reaction was going to be, I had no idea; I just hoped that it would be able to keep itself under control. There's nothing worse than vomiting in company, even if that company is about eight centimetres high and happens to have a tail and gills as well as arms and legs.

It was a hideous sight that greeted me. The wrigglers had formed a mound which seethed with activity, burrowing past each other in their efforts to feed. To begin with they looked like a mass of tails and legs, but when my guide got to them and made some high-pitched squeaking noises they ceased their activity and started to back away from what they were feeding on. And when they did, I could see that they were covered in blood from their heads down to around where I imagined their waists would be.

They formed a circle around their kill, which was some sort of large salamander, about half a metre in length. It was a sickly white colour and had been eviscerated by the wrigglers. Where its eyes should have been there were just round bumps, as if its skin had grown over the eyeballs. It had a long, almost fish-like tail and webbed feet.

I nodded at the wrigglers, who were standing around with shy, bloody smiles on their faces as if waiting for my approval.

The wriggler who had been my guide moved across to the salamander and plunged its hands into the open stomach, fiddled about for a bit, then removed a largish internal organ. It held it up to me, nodding its head with excitement.

I have to admit that the thought of eating the raw innards of a subterranean lizard didn't exactly fill me with glee, but if I didn't eat I'd starve, and then I'd be no use to the wrigglers at all. My mind conjured up a quick image of the wrigglers feeding off my corpse, but I put that out of my head as quickly as possible.

Reluctantly, I reached out and took the bloody morsel, popping it in my mouth before I had time to change my mind. My senses were immediately flooded by the same nauseating mixture of blood and fish, but I chewed quickly and swallowed, forcing myself to overcome my natural reaction to vomit.

It went down surprisingly easily, my stomach growling in eager anticipation. And, to my great surprise, I found myself wanting more.

Apart from vegetables, I'd never eaten anything raw in my whole life, not even sashimi at a Japanese restaurant, so the fact that I wanted—no, craved—more was a surprise to me. Perhaps it was because I'd been without food of any variety for so long, or possibly it was my body understanding that it had to acclimatise to a new diet, but, whatever the reason, I was eager to get on with the meal. There was going to be a small problem with that, however, as the second I'd swallowed the piece the wriggler had handed me, the entire group leapt on the carcass once again and recommenced eating. It looked like I'd be left with skin and bones.

I tried to push a few of the feeding bodies aside gently, but got my finger rather savagely bitten in the process, so I had to content myself with sitting on the sand and watching the proceedings, my hunger growing more intense every second.

They left me half and, to give them their due, it was the tail and hindquarters which contained most of the flesh. I gnawed the carcass right down to the bones, sucking each tiny morsel of flesh that was left behind.

My stomach continued to lurch and squirm uncomfortably, but for the first time in ages it felt full. The effect of the meal was almost instantaneous. Hopefully, I wouldn't be spending quite so much time asleep or in a half-daze hallucinating about fish fingers. The memory of that image made me feel extremely guilty, and every time I looked at any of the wrigglers I'd feel a rush of blood in my face and an overwhelming desire to start prattling on about any subject as long as it didn't involve food.

The wrigglers were scattered about the cave, some of them sleeping heaped together in small mounds, others arranged in strategic places along the bank of the stream. They were almost military in their precision, moving in groups up and down beside the flowing water as if they were performing sentry duty. I had no idea what their social structure was, but it appeared to be extremely close-knit and—if the dead salamander was anything to go by—brutally efficient.

Now that my belly was full and my mind functioning

again, I had time to think. I became acutely aware of my predicament: that I was isolated underground with a group of half-fish, half-human creatures, cut off from everything and everyone I'd ever known.

And on top of it all, what had happened to Edie hit me as hard as a house brick in the face.

In effect, I'd deserted her, even though it was under her instructions, left her at the mercy of the Sirs or the Americans or, even more unpleasant, the feral pigs that infested Tankworld, the strange property where we'd been trapped. More than likely, I'd saved the wrigglers from capture, but that didn't make me feel any better. Edie had saved me from a fire and dragged me half-way across Australia, teaching me a whole lot about compassion and tolerance along the way, so the debt was still weighted heavily in her favour.

Leaving her to die wasn't exactly how I'd intended to pay her back, and I was overwhelmed with an enormous sadness at my inadequacy and loss. During the time I'd known Edie, my emotions had leapt about all over the place, riding a roller-coaster from joy to pure loathing and, now that I had time to reflect, I understood there was one emotion that stood out from them all.

It was a little thing called love, and realising it made me sick to the stomach. What a thing to discover after you'd deserted someone. I would have liked to have told her before we were separated; at least then she would have known that someone cared.

I found myself sobbing uncontrollably, visions of Edie, my parents and my brother flickering silently before my eyes.

And, as I cried, the wrigglers seemed to notice. First it was the ones patrolling along the side of the stream who stopped and stared at me. Then the others started to wake up, almost as if they'd been informed somehow. As a group, they moved towards me, slowly at first, then they seemed to overcome whatever reluctance they had and they swarmed across the floor of the cave and up my torso.

My immediate reaction was to recoil, but after a few seconds I realised they meant me no harm. Quite the opposite, in fact.

The wrigglers climbed up to my chest and, in unison, began to make a low keening noise, almost a sympathetic hum. I found my sobbing begin to recede, and a low moan took its place, a moan which followed the cadences made by the wrigglers. It was our tiny song to Edie.

They clustered about on my chest, some of them tucking themselves right under my chin, their little hands reaching up and stroking my face. And we sat there for what seemed like eternity, humming sadly at our mutual loss.

From then on, time meant nothing to me. It was a concept rather than reality, something I remembered with fondness from my life before the tunnels. We slept and ate, ate and slept.

Occasionally I would drift off to sleep and wake up alone in the cave, the wrigglers having gone off to forage for food. I would always experience a moment of panic, afraid that they wouldn't come back; but they always did, leaping from the water and scuttling across the sand to greet me with their squeakings.

It was also the loneliest time of my life, even though the wrigglers tried to make it otherwise. When I was stationary, they would gather close, sitting on the stumps of my legs and looking up at me while I propped my back against the cave wall. There was a definite bond developing between us, as if the death of Edie had made us kin, cousins in sadness.

The food they brought back was far more varied than I expected, ranging from large salamanders through a variety of albino fish and small shrimp-like creatures to strange varieties of weed and mould. My initial reluctance to eat these pale and unappetising offerings soon disappeared, and I found myself joining with the wrigglers, stuffing things into my mouth without really caring what they might do to me.

If the wrigglers could eat them, then so could I. There was an old saying which my father used a lot: beggars can't be choosers. I figured I was as close to being a beggar as I'd ever been, so I gave up being choosy.

The regular food and exercise began to have a profound effect on the wrigglers. Though I had no idea how long we'd been in the cave, it quickly became obvious that it had been some time, as the tiny creatures I'd swum through the tunnel with began to grow at an astonishing rate. Before I even realised, they'd doubled in size, their human features becoming more pronounced the larger they got, their tails shrinking.

I had thought that they may have developed into replicas of human children, but this was not the case. As their fish-like features shrank away, they started to look like miniature adults. And as this happened, it became obvious that there were equal numbers of males and females in the group.

But that was the only thing that set any of them apart, because aside from their sexual differences they were identical. Uncannily so. And I could see their parents—Edie's sisters/brothers, Violet and Mauve—in each of them.

I began to realise that the wrigglers were considerably more than a loose group of alike-looking individuals. They possessed something much greater than that, a collective consciousness that provided them with an ability to sense what others in the group were doing. They were, after all, a school; and if you have ever seen a school of fish you will know exactly what I'm talking about.

Under water, fish seem to be able to move and turn

in unison, as if they are under the guidance of some greater power, operated by cosmic remote control. What I began to understand in those long, timeless months in the cave was that it was the result of group awareness. Each individual understood the intentions and directions of all the others. This did not mean that they all did exactly the same thing, but they all had a notion of what the others were doing.

If one of them got into difficulty, the others sensed it and rushed to their aid.

As I watched this, it came to me that the human race probably had a lot to learn from this behaviour. People, in the main, are too self-centred and greedy to ever consider a greater good, too full of ego and pride to be aware of others. I wondered if we had always been this way, or if it was something we had cultivated. Primitive man had been a tribal creature, individual survival inextricably linked to that of the group.

Perhaps selfishness is purely a modern phenomenon?

One time, the wrigglers and I were quite close to the bank of the stream, indulging ourselves in a feast of mighty proportions. Earlier, they'd brought back a selection of pale aquatic creatures and weeds, and we were gathered together 'scarfing' down whatever morsels took our fancy. Hunting had been extremely good.

Normally, we'd have carried the food further away from the stream to where the cave was drier, but there'd been so much collected we simply laid it out along the bank and got stuck in. Everyone was ravenously hungry, and soon the cave was filled with the sounds of smacking lips and the suck and slurp of flesh being pulled from carcasses.

It happened very quickly, too quickly for anyone to react.

One second I was savouring a particularly tasty cave shrimp, crunching happily through its outer casing to get at the sweet white meat underneath, the school clustered around me, and the next there was total confusion.

From the stream came a massive gout of water, surging up from under the surface. The cave echoed with that ghastly farting sound that I vaguely remembered from when we'd first arrived, though this time it was much louder, suffused with anger and violence. I caught a quick glimpse of something large and black erupting onto the bank, and then I toppled over onto my back, the wrigglers leaping over me in their mad panic to escape. The air was suddenly filled with their squeakings and I could feel their tiny feet and hands all over me as they ran for the back of the cave.

Oh, just leave me, I thought, thanks a heap.

I struggled over onto my side and found myself face to face with something far worse than any of my wildest nightmares.

Squatting on the bank, not half a metre from me, was something that looked like a cross between a giant spider and a scorpion. But no god in their right mind would have created something this hideous. It was a good metre long and covered with glistening black hair still dripping from the stream. It had two massive, crab-like claws at the front and a short, ugly tail tipped with a vicious spine which was raised threateningly above its back. Its head seemed to be a collection of eyes which swivelled in all directions, and in the centre of its face was a mouth totally out of proportion to the rest of it.

In one claw it held one of the wrigglers, still alive and screaming and, as I watched, it pushed it head-first into its ghastly mouth, its hundreds of teeth mashing down. I heard the crunching of bone and the wriggler thrashed briefly and was still.

From the back of the cave I heard a collective groan of pain and agony come from the rest of the school, as if they had felt every painful second of their friend's death.

As the body of the wriggler disappeared inside its mouth, vents along both sides of the creature's body opened in unison and it emitted that huge windy noise, though this time there was a definite note of triumph to the sound, the trumpeting of someone secure in their strength, confident of victory. It was like some hideous school bully after beating the crap out of someone one-third their own size.

Its many eyes glared right at me. I was frozen in place, too terrified to move, the thought of those massive claws grabbing at my face overcoming all my natural survival responses. If it had come for me right then, I would have done nothing to stop it, simply sat there while its claws ripped me apart, but for some reason it left me alone, scuttling past my prone form in pursuit of the panicking wrigglers.

It caught up to them in no time at all, wading into the school, its tail lashing about and doing massive damage to whomever it struck. I saw it lift two struggling bodies in its claws and wave them above it like bloody trophies, the wrigglers already dead from the savage pressure the claws exerted.

Everything was chaos.

I'm not sure exactly what motivated me to action, whether it was anger at the creature or fear of being left alone should all the school perish. Whatever it was, I hauled myself upright and lurched across the floor of the cave, my eyes searching frantically for a weapon of some kind. If I hadn't left the scuba tank behind in the tunnel, I may have had something heavy enough to immobilise the creature, but all that was left from my journey was the useless diving mask.

Then I had a sudden inspiration, one which came from panic rather than any rational thinking. I grabbed one of the smaller stalagmites with both hands and wrenched it away from the floor of the cave. It was astonishingly heavy and slimy with moisture, but at least it was a weapon.

The school had now turned on the creature, attack being their only defence. They hung from its every appendage, biting at it and pounding with their tiny fists, though they seemed to make little difference. The creature continued to impale them with its tail spine and wrench them from its body with its claws, tossing them willy-nilly about the cave.

Tucking the stone spear under one arm, I let out a bellow of rage and crossed the cave towards the creature.

As I reached it, almost as if they anticipated my actions, the school suddenly left off their attack on the creature and spread out in a circle around it. Momentarily confused by their actions, the creature froze, its claws and tail raised threateningly at the encircling wrigglers.

It didn't see me coming.

I only had a brief second to pull the spear from under my arm and raise it above my head in both hands like a massive dagger, before I toppled forward onto its back.

The stalagmite smashed through its hard outer casing like a rock through thin ice, passing out the other side of its body and plunging into the floor of the cave. The creature convulsed wildly, its tail catching me in the side, and I briefly felt a searing stab of pain as the spine broke through my skin and tore away a strip of flesh.

I hit the floor of the cave with a thump that caused

my vision to spin wildly.

I had a brief image of the creature impaled to the cave floor, its legs, claws and tail thrashing madly about it, and the circle of wrigglers closing in, before everything went black.

The first thought that struck me on waking was that I'd been spending a lot of time unconscious since I arrived in the cave. The second thought was that it was a welcome way of passing the time, since there was little else to do except eat and knuckle my way from one end of the place to the other.

My third thought was for the creature: what had become of it? Was it still alive? Was I the only other creature still living in the cave?

Three thoughts that qualified as one.

I seemed to be covered in some sort of warm, soft blanket, and when I raised my head I realised that it was the wrigglers, who were collapsed all over me. At least they provided the answers to some of my questions.

Carefully, so that I didn't disturb my sleeping burden, I craned my neck around and looked across to where I had last seen the creature. It was still there. Or at least its body was, the stalagmite still impaling it to the floor. All its other appendages were scattered around on the sand, lying like discarded elements of some half-finished school project.

There was no movement from the body section (not that there was a lot of pieces left to move), so I gathered that it was dead. For now, at least, the danger appeared to be over.

I tried to see if there were any dead wrigglers lying in the sand among the bits and pieces of the creature, but there was no sign of them. When I glanced down my body at their sleeping forms I could see that many of them carried wounds. Hopefully, not too many had been badly injured. Perhaps that was all the damage that had been done.

As I stared at them, a strange sensation overwhelmed me. It was like a warmth creeping through my insides, a tingling of deep affection. I sighed, feeling the beginnings of a major lump in my throat.

This is silly, I thought, you shouldn't be getting all emotional over fish.

But emotional I was, and there wasn't a thing my rational side could do about it. I imagined that this must be a taste of what it would be like to have children—weird children, but part of me nonetheless.

My sighing must have disturbed them because a couple of them raised their heads, wearily opening their eyes and looking in my direction. Then one of them smiled broadly, baring its tiny pointed teeth.

'That's not something any of us want to do again in a hurry,' it said.

I nodded in agreement.

It was several more seconds before I realised that it had spoken to me.

The sudden jerk I gave threw the sleeping wrigglers off my body and onto the sand, where they sat up and looked around in a dazed sort of way, rubbing their eyes to bring them back into focus. There were some weary squeaks of protest, but eventually they seemed to get themselves back into some sort of order—certainly more awake and sensible than I felt right at that moment.

The one that had spoken was watching my reaction curiously.

'What?' it said when I'd had time to fully register what was happening. 'Surely you didn't think we've been spending all our time just swimming about looking for your dinner?'

'You . . . you can *speak*!' I managed to splutter.

'Aw, shucks, you noticed,' it said modestly. 'It's a pretty easy thing for us to pick up when you spend all your time muttering to yourself. It was driving us mad.'

'But . . . ' I was at a loss as to what to say. During my time in the cave, I'd convinced myself that the only living thing that I would ever be able to converse with would be myself, and I'd accepted that this would eventually send me mad; that was, unless I was mad already. I had the uncomfortable sensation that what I was experiencing may have been an hallucination.

The wriggler shook its head. 'I know what you're thinking. You're not mad. I really am talking to you, and I'll be happy to have a nice long chat just as soon as we clear up this mess. We have to help the injured and prepare ourselves.'

'Prepare ourselves for what?' I said, looking back to where the dead creature's form hung like a trophy from some alien hunting lodge. 'You seem to have done a pretty good job of looking after yourselves.'

'At a cost,' the wriggler said quietly. 'You'd better come and have a look.' And with that it strode out across the sand floor, looking back over its shoulder expectantly.

I rolled over and sat up, then slowly made my way after it.

The injured were behind one of the larger stalagmites, laid out in rows as though in a hospital. It was immediately obvious that several of them were already dead, their tiny bodies small and stiff. Others had sustained savage cuts and fractures from the force of the creature's claws. Unless they received immediate attention they would probably die as well.

Though most of the injured were still conscious, not one of them moaned in pain. They bore their injuries with quiet acceptance, their faces rigid with the effort.

From what I could gather, at least one-third of the group had been hurt.

'This is terrible,' I whispered. 'We don't have anything to treat them with.'

'Then we'll just have to make do,' came the reply from the wriggler I'd been speaking to. 'We can't leave them like this. They were fighting for all of us, so we're not going to give up on them.'

'I wasn't suggesting that. It's just that . . . well, we simply don't have anything that could help them.' I looked about myself in desperation. 'There are no medicines or bandages or anything.'

'Do what you can,' the wriggler said grimly, 'and we'll see what we can find to help you.'

With that, it spun around and started squeaking wildly at the wrigglers that were still standing. About half of them immediately headed off towards the stream. The remainder started to comfort their injured companions.

'We'll be back,' the talking wriggler said as it headed off towards the stream with the others. 'They trust you now, so don't let them down.'

'And what about you?' I called after it. 'Do you trust me?'

'If one of us trusts you, we all do.' Then, just before it leapt into the water, it turned back to me again. 'By the way, you can call me Slap. You're pretty big on names, you people.'

'Slap,' I muttered to myself after they'd gone. 'I suppose that's a good enough name. For a fish.'

I turned back to the group of wounded wrigglers feeling completely useless. What could I possibly do to help them? Then I got to thinking that feeling useless was pretty useless in itself, so I moved over to them and started working by instinct.

Slap and his companions brought back long sections of weed, which we used to bind the wrigglers' wounds, and a variety of fungi that we pounded with rocks and mixed with saliva, then applied as poultices.

'If there's any poison from that sting, the fungus may help to draw it from the wounds,' Slap said as we worked. 'The sort of thing the Native Americans do in movies.'

'You've never seen a movie,' I finally replied. 'How can you know about stuff like that?'

Slap chuckled. 'I've seen every movie that my parents ever saw, read every book and know every conversation that ever passed their lips. All of us have. Apart from jumbling a few words that have similar meanings, we remember everything. It's our inheritance.'

'You never even knew them, so how can you possibly know any of that?'

'I don't know, we just do. I even know what they thought about you and Marvin.' Slap grinned and went on pounding with his rock.

I shook my head. 'Okay, you win. What did they think of me and Marvin?'

'Not a lot. They thought Marvin was an idiot who was so besotted with Edie that they could make him do pretty much anything that they wanted. And they thought you were dangerous.'

'Can't get everything right, I suppose.'

'What do you mean?'

'Marvin certainly wasn't an idiot. He pretty much knew what your parents were up to. I was the stupid one. I didn't believe him until it was almost too late. Lucky for you lot. Dangerous . . . well, who knows?'

'Yes . . . luck does play a big part in most things that are important. If it wasn't for luck, mankind certainly wouldn't have lasted as long as it has. Evolution has been nine parts luck and one part determination since the beginning.'

I put down the rock I was using and looked across at Slap. He was working with a look of concentration on his face, pounding the shreds of fungus into a paste. 'You know, for someone who hadn't said a word of English until a short time back, you've turned into something of a philosopher.'

He shrugged. 'I've got a lot of thinking to draw on, not just our parents' ideas, but everyone here as well. That's a lot of minds working on the same thoughts. I guess it's inevitable that we'd come to conclusions faster. But we've got more important things to do at present than sit here and chat about why the human race is about to come to an end. Let's see if this poultice does any good.'

And with that we returned to the task of taking care of the wounded.

I hadn't had any experience of a school intelligence. Of course, I'd done the 'going to school' bit, but that was a different thing entirely. What I was dealing with now was a group of individuals who naturally acted as one, without complaint or dissent.

We applied poultices and bandages for what seemed like hours, comforting the wounded. They'd all started speaking, now that Slap had broken the ice, and my mind whirled with the names they kept giving me: Shark, Fizzgig, Burp, Thumper, Glitter, Shampoo, Tough. It was as if someone jabbed their finger in a dictionary and randomly allocated words to them. There was no way I was going to remember them all and, since apart from sexual differences they all looked alike, putting names to faces was going to be an impossibility. But that was a problem I was going to have to face at some other time; saving lives was my current task.

Though only seven of the wrigglers had actually died, the attack by the creature had devastated the population of the cave: at least half of them carrying injuries of some kind, several of which I thought might turn out to be fatal. The injured bore their wounds with a quiet stoicism, their faces set against the pain.

The tunnels obviously supported an amazing selection of life forms, and I hoped that most of them were harmless. The creature that had attacked us had been a monstrosity from a nightmare. I prayed that it wouldn't be a recurring one. Though it had recognisable features, it was a mixture I had never seen before, and I wondered what could have caused the mutation. I didn't think for a second that it had been a natural product of evolution.

What else was quietly mutating deep underground? What other horrors were we likely to come face to face with? I didn't want to think about it, but my mind has a habit of running away with itself, and every now and then it would pull me up short with another horrific image that it had created without my help.

Slap, on the other hand, was high-spirited and full of beans.

The success with the creature had obviously made him feel relatively indestructible, which I thought was a dangerous state of mind. One victory, after all, does not win a war. I had the horrible feeling that the appearance of the creature had been little more than an exploratory incursion, a scout from a much larger force.

Every now and then I'd hear Slap whistling a slightly familiar tune, which I eventually recognised as 'We Are The Champions' by that stone-age band, Queen.

'You seem rather happy, all things considered,' I said to him the next time he was nearby. Slap was easy to recognise. He'd tied a strip of weed around his forehead, so that he looked like a miniature version of one of those Japanese Kamikaze pilots from the Second World War.

'Well, why not?' he replied chirpily. 'We won, didn't we? With a lot of help from you. And our losses have been quite minor. We're all feeling very positive at the moment.'

'You don't want to start getting too cocky,' I said, as I tightened a weed bandage on the arm of one of the wounded wrigglers. 'That used to be my problem, and you can see where it got me. It's good that we defeated it, but you have to realise that there may be more of them. I mean, what would happen if a half dozen of the damn things suddenly popped up out of the stream right now?'

Slap looked over his shoulder with a sudden expression of fear. 'You don't really think that more of them are coming, do you?'

'I don't know,' I said. 'But if there's one, then there simply have to be others. How did it get there in the first place? Something had to give birth to it. It had parents. You'd better start making some plans. Otherwise we'll be up that famous creek without a paddle.' I thought for a second. 'Or under it, as the case seems to be.'

Slap looked across at me and nodded briefly, then he scampered off and began gesturing animatedly to some of the other more mobile wrigglers.

I hope he knows what he's doing, I thought, as the group made their way to the stream and disappeared from view.

How long the group was away I have no idea, as I was too concerned with the injured to notice the passing of time, but their return caused some consternation.

They erupted from the stream in a flurry of panicking bodies and cries of alarm. Several had to be helped from the water, and even from a distance I could see that we would be dealing with more injured. As I made my way towards them with the others, I hoped that Slap had come through all right. Then I noticed his Kamikaze headband bobbing about amongst the crowd of wrigglers and heard his voice squeaking orders.

He broke off and turned to me as I reached the group. 'You were right,' he gasped out, 'there are more of them. Lots more. They caught us by surprise about half a kilometre away. It was as if they knew we were coming.'

'Maybe you aren't the only things around who instinctively know what everyone else in their school is thinking,' I replied.

'They're not like us!' Slap almost snarled at me. 'How can you even think that?'

'That's not quite what I meant. I just thought they might be able to sense things like you lot.' I looked across at the freshly injured. 'Anyway, there's no time to stand around discussing semantics. I presume they're coming this way?'

This time Slap grinned. 'Not for a while, I wouldn't think. They may have caught us by surprise, but we gave a lot more than we got. One thing these creatures can't do is manoeuvre well in the tunnels, especially where they get narrow. There are now a couple of their dead mates blocking the way down here, but I'm not sure how long that's going to hold them up.'

I swore loudly. It was perhaps not the most articulate of replies, but it pretty much summed up how I felt about the situation. If there was a large group of the creatures coming, staying in the cave would be suicide. Once a large force of them made it out of the stream, they'd run riot in the open spaces, mowing wrigglers down like so many blades of grass. (I suddenly had the strangest thought, right out of the blue, and totally unrelated to anything. I realised with perfect clarity that I hadn't seen grass for what seemed like years, not since Edie and I had made it to Tankworld all that time ago. And I feared that it would be very unlikely that I'd ever see it again.)

'That's an intelligent response,' Splash suddenly said, interrupting my thoughts. I was once again back in ugly reality.

'Sorry,' I muttered.

'Should we make a stand along the stream?' he asked. 'We might be able to hold them if we can stop them getting out of the water.'

I could almost picture the scene, the blood flowing downstream as the wrigglers and creatures locked each other in combat along the bank. There would be a chance of victory, a small one, but that would be short-lived. The creatures would just re-group and keep coming, until eventually they would overwhelm the wrigglers.

'No,' I finally said, 'that would be disastrous. We're going to have to get out of here.'

Splash considered this for a moment, then asked, 'But how are you going to come with us? You can't breathe under water.'

'I hadn't thought of that.'

The solution was definitely original.

Naturally, I'd offered to sacrifice myself by remaining behind while the wrigglers swam off to safety. I figured that was expected of me, even if I knew deep down that they wouldn't leave me behind. The suggestion was dismissed without even discussion.

'No way. That option doesn't exist,' Slap said. 'The only reason we're here is because of you and Edie. We're not going to desert you just because it's an easy solution.'

I didn't argue.

'There must be some way we can assist you to breathe,' he went on. 'It's a matter of transferring air from us to you. It's just physics.'

'I was never very good at physics,' I mumbled. 'But I still don't see how it's possible.'

'If we're possible,' someone else said, 'anything's possible.' This brought a round of chuckling to the group, and I felt myself relaxing a little.

'What if one of us stuck our head in his mouth and breathed out?' came a suggestion.

'Oh, gross,' another voice added. 'Have you smelt his breath lately?' More laughter. Then silence.

'It's worth a try,' Slap said slowly. 'It's about the only option we have, and it might just work.' He looked across at me and winked. 'Just don't sneeze, otherwise you'll probably decapitate me.'

We entered the stream in waves. A force of the strongest and fittest went first, followed by the injured, then finally another group of wrigglers who were still pretty mobile along with myself.

As I held my breath and the cold water closed over my head, I almost panicked and backed out, my confidence in Slap's ability to keep my lungs functioning not high at all. It was a strange, almost parasitic method of survival, and the image of myself with a wriggler hanging out of my mouth was almost too much to contemplate. But I didn't have that many choices in the matter.

It was very dark. Though after a while I could make out the shapes of the wrigglers swimming around me, and I realised that they had developed some slight luminescence of their own, probably from eating the fungus which grew through the cave.

The light made the journey more bearable, but not much.

Then my lungs started to make themselves known and I signalled madly at Slap.

We'd worked out what to do before entering the water, but this was the first time we were going to try it out. The method was simple: I'd gradually let most of the air out of my lungs, then Slap would shove his head into my mouth while I sealed my lips around his throat. Then he'd breathe out into my mouth, hopefully providing enough air for me to survive on.

I felt like a lion at the circus, about to take the tamer's head between my jaws.

The act itself was grotesque and unpleasant, one of the reasons being that Slap's head only just managed to fit in my mouth, and locks of his hair caught at the back of my throat. I almost choked to death before I realised that air had entered my lungs, and when I pulled Slap free from my mouth it was like trying to remove what felt like a gigantic hair ball.

I swallowed some water, but overall the technique seemed to achieve the desired results. Slap peered closely at me as I signalled that it was okay, then we continued to swim back down the underground tunnel.

Lit by the faint luminescence of the wrigglers, the

tunnel was smooth and undulating. It felt like I had been transported into a passageway constantly traversed by gigantic worms or some such creatures which sanded the walls with their flesh.

After several tries at the buddy-breathing technique, Slap and I had it down to a fine art. Each time I 'borrowed' air from him, it was enough to last me for close to a minute, as long as I didn't thrash about too much and use up all the oxygen in my lungs. Once we'd mastered it, we tended to make fairly good time, which was a blessing, as we didn't know how long it would take for the nightmare creatures to break through the barrier the wrigglers had created earlier and come charging down the tunnel at us.

We were heading back to a branch in the tunnel which would, according to the wrigglers, lead us away from the creatures to another system of caves where we should be safe.

I vaguely remembered the side branch from when we'd first come in from that direction, but at the time I'd been too concerned about surviving to pay it any attention. The reason I'd ignored it on the way through was because it had looked smaller than the tunnel I was already in, and that didn't seem to offer much hope of salvation. Slap, however, said it led through to another cavern, even larger than the one we'd been living in.

The way back was partially blocked by the old scuba tank I'd used to get through the waterways in the first place, and I had to push it in front of me until we finally made it to the side branch. It was like discovering a fragment of a past life, one which brought with it both sadness and joy. For a second I almost dragged it after me when we turned off the main tunnel, but decided it would be too much effort. And at that stage of my life I really didn't need to be hauling memories after me like so much baggage.

I'm glad I left it where it was. If I hadn't, the Americans would have found us, and the wrigglers would have spent the rest of their lives in observation tanks in some hidden laboratory.

As it was, the disaster that had driven us from our first place of refuge ended up being our salvation.

9

Another cave, another chance at some sort of life.

Having successfully negotiated the tunnels using Slap as breathing apparatus, we emerged from the water into what was a larger version of the cave where the scorpion attacked us. The roof was high, the floor soft virgin sand and mineral deposits interspersed with glowing fungus, stalagmites and stalactites.

'Deja vu,' I gasped when I could finally speak again.

'What's that?' Slap replied. 'Some band from the eighties?'

I laughed until my sides hurt.

'You may have inherited your parents' memories,' I finally managed to chuckle back at him, 'but you got Edie's sense of humour.'

'I don't see that I've said anything funny.' Slap sounded insulted by my outburst and stomped off with some of the other wrigglers to explore the cave. I felt like calling out to him that I was just joking, but I didn't think that it would help. Any statement that made fun of his parents was bound to upset him . . . bound to upset all of them, since anything that affected one affected the group. I'd have to be especially careful about what I said.

I rolled about in the sand to dry myself off then made

my way slowly around the perimeter of the cave, checking about for signs that it may have been occupied at any stage by the scorpions, or anything else for that matter. What I thought I'd find I have no idea, as I'd never seen any place the scorpions had inhabited, but I figured that if I found anything that looked out of place it would trigger alarms.

Nothing did. The cave was as unoccupied as the last.

'SANCTUARY!' I bellowed in my best Hunchback of Notre Dame voice, 'SANCTUARY!'

My shouting brought the wrigglers running from all corners of the cave, their faces alight with alarm. They found me propped against a stalagmite, giggling to myself.

'What's up with you?' Slap asked, a look of concern on his face.

'I'm Lord of the Fish,' I cackled, 'headmaster of the school, Aquaboy, the great fishbreath.' Everything suddenly seemed so funny I couldn't stop laughing. It was as if someone had been playing an incredibly elaborate joke on me my entire life, that any second I'd find myself back in bed at my parents' house with both legs functioning and my brother hammering on the door to tell me that breakfast was ready.

None of this is real, I thought, I've just been dreaming. There's no way I just negotiated a water-filled tunnel with a fish stuck in my mouth to breathe. I have not just had an encounter with some form of mutant scorpion. I have not sawn my legs off with a hacksaw and left the person I love to die out on the Nullarbor. This is just not happening.

'You're off your nut, aren't you?' Slap said, his look of concern changing to one that suggested I'd just farted in church.

'No,' I said, 'just letting off stress.'

'What have you got to be stressed about? I just spent the last half an hour peering at your tonsils. If anyone needs to let off stress it's me,' he replied.

I grinned. 'Go right ahead.'

And then they all started giggling along with me.

Like their advanced rate of growth, the wrigglers' recuperative powers were astonishing. Within days of our migration to the new cave, even the most seriously injured of them were up and about, taking short swims along the stream to further aid their recovery. Wounds that were deep and open when we arrived were now little more than scar tissue, and broken bones had knit completely, leaving only the occasional wince or slight limp as a reminder. It was easy for me now to understand the Americans' interest in the wrigglers; they were much more than just creatures who could exist equally well in and out of fresh water, they were almost superhuman in their ability to grow and survive.

We now had sentries permanently posted at the branch off the main tunnel and the two smaller entries to the cave. At least if the scorpions decided to follow us we'd have some decent warning before they attacked, and a much better chance of defending ourselves should that happen.

By way of weaponry, I'd snapped off several of the larger stalagmites for myself and an array of smaller ones for the wrigglers. They weren't much but they were better than nothing. I'd also positioned several large pieces off some gigantic stalagmites which had already collapsed (years ago I hoped) along the edge of the stream. If a large attack came I'd use them to create a blockage where the main branch of the stream entered the cave, which should give us time to make our escape by one of the smaller entrances.

We'd send teams of wrigglers out exploring these other routes to see where they led, and early reports were promising. It appeared that the smaller streams led to even more caves and tunnels, going off in all directions. There'd be plenty of places to run to should anything bad happen. It's good to have options.

Something which began worrying me around that time was the fact that, by escaping the scorpions, we had managed to get ourselves closer to where we'd first started, at the cave back at Tankworld. And even though we were still quite some distance from it, the thought of pursuit from that direction began to niggle at the edges of my mind. I had no real idea of how we'd cope should the Americans send people after us, as they'd be a lot smarter than a group of hungry arachnids.

It occurred to me that I'd probably be a lot better off by simply giving up to them, but by doing that I'd be betraying Edie's trust, and I wouldn't do that in a million years. I'd also be betraying the wrigglers, who'd end up spending the rest of their lives as specimens or breeding stock or whatever else the powers that be had in mind for them. It just wasn't right.

Slap must have had some idea of what was going through my mind. He made a point of seeking me out when I was off in a corner of the cave chipping away at a sliver of rock in a clumsy attempt to create some form of stone knife. I'd seen it done on some TV documentary about primitive man in Africa, and figured that, if a mob of Neanderthals who hadn't even invented the wheel yet could do it, then so could I. After taking all the skin off my knuckles and losing a fingernail, I began to think that maybe they weren't quite so stupid after all.

'Good with your hands, are you?' he asked, walking up behind me.

I wasn't in any mood for sarcasm. 'No. I was just giving myself a manicure.'

'Looks a lot like you're trying to do the same thing to your fingers that you did to your legs, only not so neat. You want me to send someone back to Tankworld to retrieve the hacksaw?' Slap seemed to be in a boisterous mood.

'What are you so damn gleeful about.' Now that he was here I could put down my excuse for a knife without feeling too disgraced. I didn't think I'd try any more stone tools for a while.

'Don't let me stop you,' he went on, grinning.

'Oh, shut up,' I said, an embarrassed grin replacing my attempt at sternness. I dipped my fingers in the stream to wash off the blood. 'Come on, out with it. What's up?'

I thought Slap's grin would split his face in half. 'When's your hatchday?'

'What?'

'You heard me.'

'What the hell's a hatchday when it's at home?'

Now it was Slap's turn to look embarrassed. 'You know . . . what do you call it? When your parents hatched you.'

'*Birth*day.'

'That's the one. I knew it was something like that. When is it?'

'October 28th. Why?'

Slap grinned shyly. 'Well, we figured that, with the way things are down here, not knowing if it's day or night, even when it is, we'd make today whatever your birthday is. You know, sort of start everything off fresh from there.'

'Why my birthday?'

'So we could have a party, of course, dummy. A

birthday party cum thank you party for everything you've done for us. Don't think we're not grateful for everything you've given up for our sakes.'

I was speechless.

'So what do you reckon?' he asked, after I'd sat with my mouth open for an inordinately long period of time.

'We don't have any hats or candles,' I finally muttered, perhaps a little ungraciously.

'You'd look silly in a hat.'

The wrigglers' idea of a surprise was to make me sit at the far end of the cave with my face to the wall for several hours while they made all the arrangements. There were two wrigglers stationed on either side of me to make sure I didn't peek, a task they took to with great enthusiasm. If I so much as sighed they'd be instantly alert, looks of stern disapproval on their faces.

'If you turn round you'll spoil the surprise,' one of them squeaked when I moved slightly to ease the massive cramp I'd developed in my right buttock. It's not easy sitting facing a stone wall for hours at a time.

'Oh, give me a break, I'm just getting comfortable,' I whimpered.

'Plenty of time for that later,' came the answer. 'Slap said you weren't to move.'

'I'm sure he just meant for me to stay here, not remain frozen in place.'

'He said to make sure you didn't move a muscle, and you've been doing that constantly. You're not very good at obeying orders, are you?'

'And I don't think you're very good at interpreting them,' I shot back.

Luckily for us, Slap chose that moment to return, otherwise I think I might have ended up losing my temper in a major way.

'Hey guys,' he chirped, 'ready to party?'

'Thank the Lord,' I exclaimed as I fell back from the wall. 'These little fascists of yours have had me standing stock still from the moment you left. If I had legs they'd have up and left me in protest.'

'But you don't have any, so stop your whingeing.'

'Oh, thanks for the sympathy. That wasn't quite the reply I was expecting on my birthday.'

We were still griping at each other as we joined all the other wrigglers, who had formed themselves in a large circle around a massive pile of glowing fungus, which they must have gathered from several other caves. It was the biggest party candle I'd ever seen and it gave off quite a spectacular amount of light, making that area of the cave appear, just for a moment, like it was lit for a major celebration. Which, I guess, it was. Not only was it to celebrate my birthday (which could have come and gone several times for all I knew, I'd lost track ages ago), but it also marked the beginning of time for us, the point where we consciously drew a line and said 'our lives together start from here'.

Up until then, we'd felt we were living on borrowed time. Survival was the only thing that was clear to us. Now, however, it felt like things were different, as if we'd all suddenly decided to take control of our lives rather than have them directed by others.

It suddenly felt like we weren't running any more.

There was silence as I took my place in the ring of wrigglers. Then Slap lifted his arms above his head and whispered to me, 'Be nice, we've been practising this.' And as he dropped his arms to his sides again, they all burst into a heartfelt version of 'Happy Birthday'.

I was so touched I burst into tears when they started the 'hip hip hooray' bit at the end.

'I know our singing isn't exactly wonderful,' Slap said when he saw me crying, 'but I didn't think it was bad enough to warrant tears.'

'The singing's just wonderful,' I literally sobbed, my voice torn to pieces by emotion, 'it's the nicest thing I've ever heard.'

'But you're crying anyway . . . ?'

'It'll happen to you one day, you mark my words.'

'I doubt it,' Slap said, sounding extremely sure of himself. 'You ever heard of a fish crying?'

He had a good point. I grinned at him weakly.

'You ready to party now?' he asked.

'Ready as I'll ever be.'

And party we did.

Since the wrigglers didn't have a CD player handy, they created their own music, regaling me with the selection of songs they'd inherited from their parents. It wasn't exactly my style of entertainment, as I'm more of a Blues kind of guy, but they did a pretty good job, all things considered.

They'd also spent the time I was facing the wall gathering heaps of cave shrimp and other delicacies they knew I was fond of, so we all feasted and sang through two entire sentry shifts. I hadn't had that much fun since . . . well, since I used to go on those early morning runs with Edie and Marvin, back when things were sort of normal.

Eventually, I was so stuffed with food the very thought of another shrimp was enough to make me feel ill, and my throat was hoarse from singing. There were wrigglers flaked out all over the place, replete and exhausted, the scene looking like the aftermath of some major battle, except everyone was wearing bits of weeds around their heads and arms as stand-in party decorations.

I felt incredibly happy, and delighted by the fact that I'd outlasted even the hardest partying wrigglers.

Pretty good for an old bloke, I thought. Well, old compared to the rest of the partygoers.

'What are you looking so smug about?' a voice piped up next to my right ear. It was Slap, who was lying on his back with half a gnawed shrimp in his hand. His weed headband had slipped down so that it covered his right eye, making him look like a drunk pirate, but he didn't seem to notice.

'I'm just happy, that's all. And impressed by my staying abilities. I've outlasted the lot of them,' I said, swinging my arm around to indicate the sleeping wrigglers.

'Except me,' smiled Slap. He looked at the shrimp in his hand with mild disgust, burped quietly and tossed it behind him. 'But only just. I feel like I'm about to explode.'

'Ditto.'

And we lay like that for a while, exchanging pleasantries and quietly passing wind, surrounded by the gentle snoring of the wrigglers.

I must have fallen asleep, because the next thing I knew water was splashing on my face and there were wrigglers squeaking frantically at Slap, who was sitting up and rubbing his eyes, trying to understand what they were telling him.

He seemed to wake up very quickly, though, so I knew the news wasn't good.

'What? What?' I kept saying, and he raised his hand to silence me.

The wrigglers who'd splashed water everywhere were, I realised, sentries who had been on duty while the party had been winding down. From their frantic gesturing off towards the wall of the cave where the stream entered, something had to be happening back in the tunnel. I was about to move over to where I'd stationed the boulder trap, thinking that, if there were scorpions making their way into our new cave, I'd be able to take out quite a few of them before they even knew what was happening, when Slap suddenly shouted after me, 'Zac! Zac, it's not what you think.'

I spun around. 'What is it? What's going on?'

He stared at me for a long while, then said in a whisper, 'There are lights in the tunnel. A long way off, but they're coming this way.'

It just didn't compute in my mind. For some reason I kept trying to work out how the scorpions could possibly rig up lights, and why in the hell they'd do it in the first place, when Slap supplied the answer for me.

'It's the Americans, Zac. The lights are coming from the direction of Tankworld.'

By now all the wrigglers were awake and frantic. They'd been prepared to face the scorpions without too much fuss, as they'd met and defeated them before, but the Americans were something of an unknown quantity. And a lot scarier too, as fear of them had become a race memory, inherited from Violet and Mauve. To the wrigglers it would be like some horror out of mythology suddenly come to life.

'I'm going to take a look,' I said, moving towards the edge of the stream. 'I can hold my breath back to the tunnel branch, so no-one has to come with me.'

'You're not going to leave us, are you?' Slap asked, his voice all quiet and uncertain.

'Don't be ridiculous,' I replied. 'You think I've come this far with you just so I can scoot with the first American that comes along. They *owe* me for Edie. They couldn't get me away from you lot with a crowbar.'

'I think they may have something a bit more sophisticated than that,' he said grimly. 'Wait up, I'm coming with you.'

Slap and I eased ourselves into the cold water, and as it closed over our heads I thought, here we go again.

10

After the twilight glow of the cave, the pitch darkness of the underwater tunnel was all encompassing, folding around me like thick cushions of night.

Holding my breath, I pulled myself the ten or so metres until I found the main stream and carefully eased my head into it. Peering left and right, I saw nothing. Maybe the sentry had made a mistake? I could feel Slap swirling the water close to my right ear, and after a few seconds I felt his hand tapping against the side of my face.

Turning in that direction once again, I suddenly discovered I could make out his shape hovering in mid stream. There had to be a source of light coming from behind him, but it was faint and distant. And there was something else, too, a vague sensation or vibration coming through the water.

I held myself as still as possible, hanging in the flow of the stream, the breath starting to ache in my lungs, senses all on full alert. What was it? Where was it? And then it struck me. It was the vibration made by a large motor or generator operating a long way off, gradually filtered away to almost nothing by the earth, rock and water. But it was definitely a motor, which suggested this expedition into our territory was not a fly-by-night operation.

It had to be the Americans, no-one else would go to all that trouble to find us, and short of collapsing the tunnel we were in I couldn't think of any way to stop them following. Any diving team they sent down would search every branch of the cave system for clues to our whereabouts, and since this was the first off-shoot of the main stream it was logical they'd try this place.

With my free hand I signalled at Slap's shape to head back to the cave. Just as I was about to follow him, I caught sight of a shape further along the tunnel from where we were, something oddly irregular and man-made which stood out from the smooth meanderings of the walls.

Only as I frantically dragged myself back towards the cave, my lungs rapidly running out of oxygen, did it register. It was the scuba tank I'd nearly dragged after me when we returned.

The kernel of an idea began to take root in my mind, and as I broke the surface of the stream back in the cave, dragging in a welcome lungful of air, I shouted, 'SLAP!'

It was a long shot, but our only one. Failure would guarantee capture.

Slap and a half dozen of the strongest wrigglers had swum off up the tunnel to perform two tasks.

Firstly, they had to drag my old scuba tank further up the tunnel, but not too far. It had to be close enough to the branch in the main stream that divers would still be able to see it with their lights. Hopefully it would be enough of a clue for them to follow, thinking that if my tank ended up there then the wrigglers and I must be beyond it.

Secondly, when the divers made it to the cave where we battled the scorpion, the team of wrigglers was to briefly show itself, then swim off in panic, leading the divers further away from us and, ideally, into a meeting with the scorpions. The team of wrigglers then had to get back past the divers and rejoin us, which was probably the hardest part of the exercise, though Slap seemed quietly confident that they could carry it out.

The scorpion encounter was something of a wild card, but since I only had two cards to play I was trying everything I could.

The remaining wrigglers and I stayed at the far end of our cave. We'd removed every trace of our stay, sweeping the sand with bunches of weeds to hide footprints and stuffing what supplies we could into waterproof bags made from the bladders of salamanders.

If our diversions failed and the Americans still tried to enter our refuge, the wrigglers were going to head off along one of the smaller tunnels they'd been scouting and keep going until there was no sign of pursuit. They would have a fairly good chance of escape if the Americans could be held up here, and the only thing that could do that was myself.

Since we'd been in the cave the wrigglers had continued to grow at their astonishing rate, and it was now impossible for me to use one of them to get air. It would have been like attempting to stuff a hairy softball into my mouth, which was not something I really wanted to try. (I also have the sneaking suspicion that the wrigglers were even happier about this fact than I was, but they were far too polite to mention it.)

The moment I saw light coming down the tunnel into the cave, I was going to collapse the rock pile and keep tossing stuff down on them until they either stopped or overwhelmed me. None of us had said anything about this, as we were all hoping that my first plan would work, but there was an unspoken agreement that, should this fail, I was to be sacrificed.

It was the least I could do for Edie.

Artificial light has an entirely different quality to natural luminescence. It is harsher and more yellow, and shines rather than glows.

Slap and his team had been gone for over half an hour before we began to see the first signs that divers had made it to the branch in the main stream. It was eerie.

To begin with, it appeared as if the luminescence in the cave had decided to give up the ghost after hundreds of years of happily glowing away. It just seemed to fade before our eyes, and I could hear the wrigglers murmuring darkly amongst themselves.

'Quiet!' I whispered. 'Sound travels a long way through water.'

Which is exactly when we heard the odd clanging of metal against rock, the sound of scuba tanks banging against the roof of the main stream. It was faint, but getting closer. And with the sound came a different form of light, a yellow beam which lit the area where the tunnel entered our cave. The divers had to be at the stream branch, deciding whether to explore our off-shoot or continue, at least one of them shining a torch in our direction.

Please Slap, I thought, make sure the old tank is close enough for them to see it, otherwise I'll be forced to drop large rocks on Americans, which probably won't make them very happy. I'd be a lot happier if they got pissed off at scorpions.

Then the torch glow suddenly got a lot brighter.

'They're coming this way,' I whispered. 'Get ready to go.'

Leaving the wrigglers at the far end of the cave, I lurched across to my pile of rocks and prepared to make my final stand. And it would be final if they entered the cave, I'd have nowhere else to go. The rocks teetered precariously under my hands. All it would take was a tiny push to send the lot tumbling down on the first unfortunate diver's head.

And as the light increased I began to hear more noises. Apart from the banging of the scuba tanks, I could also hear what sounded like distorted voices, as if a computer was speaking.

They must have microphones inside their masks, I decided. I'd seen diving masks like that before on nature programs, so I knew the divers must be communicating amongst themselves and the others back at their command post underneath Tankworld.

Then the approaching beam of light stopped dead.

I held my breath, listening to the distorted crackle of electrical voices and the uncertain banging of the tanks.

Please, I prayed silently, pleeease see the other tank.

And then the light started to fade. It was a slow process as the diver would have had to gradually back up along the tunnel to the main stream, there not being enough room to turn around, especially in full diving gear.

Eventually, the cave returned to its naturally luminous state, and I let out a sigh of relief, all trace of the American divers fading off up the main stream.

It was a mistake.

As I leant against the pile of boulders I'd planned to

collapse on the divers, my weight did just that, toppling the entire structure over and carrying me with it into the stream. I hit the water in a tangle of arms and rocks, struggling desperately to stay out of the way of the boulders.

When I surfaced, wet and scraped but alive, the wrigglers were running along the side of the stream to my aid, some of them already diving into the water in case I was trapped under the surface.

'You were supposed to run if I pushed these over,' I spluttered. 'You're all disobeying orders.'

'You didn't exactly push them over, did you? The divers have gone, anyway,' one of the wrigglers said as they helped me from the water. 'But we all may have to leave now.'

I lay face down on the sand to recover my breath. 'Why?' I finally gasped.

'Because your rock pile has gone and sealed the entrance,' came the answer. 'This cave's going to start filling up real soon.'

Looking back over my shoulder I could see that he was right, the boulders were piled all over the entrance. 'Oh no,' I said quietly, 'what about Slap and the others?'

Water was already starting to rise up over the edge of the stream bed and flood out across the sand of the cave floor.

An hour later there wasn't a dry spot in the entire cave, the water already reaching my knees. At the rate it was filling up I reckoned on three, maybe four hours before I either got out of the cave or learned how to breathe under water, both of which were extremely remote possibilities.

It was just about then that Slap suddenly reappeared, bobbing back to the surface just near where the boulders blocked the stream.

'What the hell are you up to,' he called out over the sound of the stream filling out into the cave. 'I nearly broke my back squeezing through those boulders. The cave's going to fill up, there's not enough room for the stream to get out properly.'

All around him other wrigglers were surfacing, all of them looking exhausted, then suddenly shocked at what was happening in the cave.

'Gee,' I replied sarcastically, 'we didn't realise that. We thought you'd be pleased at the renovations.'

'Are you nuts?' he spat.

'Totally certifiable,' I replied. 'Where are the divers?'

'Gone.' He swam up to me, still looking puzzled. 'We did what you said, waited until they made it to the other cave, then showed ourselves. They thought they'd surprised us. You should have seen the stuff these guys had. There were these little sled things they used to propel them through the water, and their face masks were all glass. They could talk to each other, Zac!'

'Yeah, we figured that one out. Go on.'

'Anyway, they came after us up the stream. Those sleds move like greased lightning, it was hard staying ahead of them. We led them up as far as the spot where the scorpions came from. It's a pit in the floor of the stream. We managed to hide up along the roof like underwater bats. They swam straight down into the pit, never even thought to look up.'

'And?'

'And then we came back here and spent forever trying to worm our way through those stupid boulders. What did you think you were doing?'

I felt like an idiot. After everything going exactly as we'd planned, I'd gone and ruined our advantage by not paying attention to what I was doing.

'I slipped,' I muttered. 'So you don't know what happened to the divers? What if they come back when they don't find you?'

Slap shook his head emphatically. 'They won't be going anywhere. Just before we reached the branch in the tunnel I started to taste blood in the water. It was just a trace, but for it to have travelled back that far, there must have been a lot of it to start off with. They're scorpion food, Zac, forget about them.'

'When they don't return they'll send others after them.'

'Yeah, so what. They'll only find what the scorpions left. And this tunnel's blocked now, as far as anything bigger than us is concerned.' Slap looked at me sadly. 'You're stuck here, you realise.'

'Possibly.'

He glared at me and slapped at the rising water with both hands. I laughed, which only made it worse. Slap looked like an angry midget stuck in a hot tub. Everything the wrigglers had stored for the trip further up the secondary tunnels was now floating in the water around us and Slap was forced to keep pushing things out of the way to talk to me.

'You're going to drown, damn you, stop laughing,' he finally spluttered at me.

'Guess what I've been thinking about?' I finally managed to gasp out when my laughter finally died away.

'What?'

'Bladders,' I said with enormous enthusiasm.

Slap stared at me like I'd finally gone totally off my nut. He thought I was standing up to my knees in water talking about taking a quick slash.

'Bladders full of . . .' I pushed one of the floating food

containers away with my hand.

'Air,' he finished for me, comprehension finally hitting him.

11

And so we left that cave, like we left the one before that. The bladders were emptied of food, and though they only supplied a small amount of air each, the wrigglers were able to keep filling them for me as we went, supplying enough air for me to reach caves farther and farther along the system.

A couple of days after we'd begun our nomadic existence, when we were already several caves away from where the Americans nearly found us, a series of distinct rumbles filled the tunnel system, shaking the earth and collapsing stalagmites all around. I figured it was either an earthquake or the Americans deciding they'd had enough of fish people and scorpions so they blew up the cave at Tankworld. Either way, we never saw or heard them again.

I guess with everything else going on in the world at that time they had more than enough to worry about. I wonder if somewhere in a long-abandoned military facility over in what's left of the good old US of A there's a file which still records our existence. Which tells a strange story of experiments by a couple of New Zealand ichthyologists and a fire in a research laboratory.

I doubt it, but you never know.

Our travels through the caves are now the stuff of legends, each adventure a part of our oral folk law. It is good to have created history.

From the time of my sudden birthday party and our resumption of taking stock of the days, close to five years passed before our return to the surface. Five years in which the wrigglers grew quickly to their full size, adapting to life underground as if it was what they were born for.

I can still remember the day when Slap came to me with the news that they'd found the source of the entire underground water system, a gap through which he said natural light streamed down.

'It's the surface, Zac,' he said to me, his eyes filling with tears. 'We can go back, maybe even find your family or something.'

But you can't go back. Things are never the same again.

And I should have taken more care, once again.

I had grown so used to life underground, so set in thinking that I'd never see the sky again, that I hurried our return, thinking the sooner I felt the sun again the better.

Apart from some food and tools we'd fashioned over the years, we simply dumped everything and set out along the tunnels. It took two hours to get there, but when we did arrive I knew I'd never be able to stay where I was for a second longer.

We were in a tiny cave, so small that most of the others had to remain under water clinging grimly to whatever they could. The current was tremendous, flooding down from the surface at an incredible rate of knots. But there was also a degree of natural light filling the cave, filtering through the water.

'This is as far as I've gone,' Slap shouted at me over the roar of the current. 'But you can see what I mean, with all that light it's got to mean there's a gap just up ahead. We're going to have to pull ourselves along from here, the current's too strong to swim against. Are you up for this?'

'Are you joking,' I shouted back, 'I've never been more ready for anything in my life. I don't ever want to see another cave again as long as I live.'

'Which may not be too long at all if it's a big swim to the surface,' he said, grinning at me.

I realised then just how much I cared for him, cared for all of them.

'If I don't make it, I just want to say ...'

'Don't say it,' Slap interrupted. 'Tell me on the surface.'

'Have it your own way,' I replied, then let go of the rock I was holding and forced my way into the current.

It was a close call.

We rounded the bend in the rock and from then on it was chaos. Two of the wrigglers grabbed me under each arm and swam for all they were worth, holding onto rocks as they went. The water was moving past me so fast it simply became a blur of hideous noise and flashing light.

Everything became surreal and disjointed, the air screaming for release from my lungs.

And then suddenly it was stillness.

I was still moving fast, but now there was no current forcing us backwards, the water getting steadily clearer and brighter.

A great golden orb appeared above me, blurred and watery, but quickly gaining definition as we neared the surface.

And then, just as my lungs decided they'd had enough and expelled everything they contained in preparation for a flood of water, my face broke the surface and the sun hit my eyes at full strength for the first time in five years.

The weirdest thing filled my ears at that moment, a song I hadn't heard for so long I thought I must have been hallucinating. Just before the pain in my eyes caused me to start screaming, I heard the long-dead Frank Zappa exclaim, 'Great Googlymoogly!'

I didn't go blind immediately, that took about three months. But there was no way to stop it, the damage I'd done by staring straight at the sun was irreparable.

In that time, though, I absorbed everything I could about our new environment, mediated between the first humans I'd seen in years and the race we now call the Originals.

The song I'd heard came from a portable tape player one of the people living by the lake had been operating. Its batteries have been dead now for years, but for some reason the great Googlymoogly tag stuck, and it's become another nickname, like Halftrack used to be when I was with Edie.

By the time my sight went completely, I had the layout of Endsville worked out in my head, and the others have been building it ever since, cohabiting and breeding a community in which everyone is accepted for who they are, as long as they are prepared to accept everyone else.

Compared to what we had all been through, life in Endsville has been relatively good to us until now. Until the Cyclists came and decided to take it from us.

PART THREE

WHERE WE'RE GOING

12

The Cyclists have been working themselves up into a frenzy, the air ringing with that weird ululation which rises higher and higher the more excited they get. I'd be lying if I told you it wasn't frightening. Because it is. It makes the hairs stand up all over my body and the blood freeze solid in my veins.

I'm not alone.

The trick is not to show it to the Cyclists. And, even more importantly, to those around me. If the great Googlymoogly himself starts to fart quietly in fear, the stink from here will rapidly become eye-watering and spread down to those who are watching the Cyclists get ready to charge.

Of my generals, only Anne remains with me. Rainbow has just left to take command of the front lines. He was so keyed up when he went I could hear his teeth grinding in anticipation. Though his bluntness can be annoying at times, I'm glad I'm on his side. I really wouldn't want to be opposing him.

'Here they come,' Anne says unnecessarily.

You can already hear the sound of the bikes hissing across the hard-packed desert sand, adding to the raised cry of the charging Cyclists.

'Is everyone where they should be? Will they stand firm?'

'There's no point in running, is there?' she replies.

There's nowhere left to run, no place that will sustain life the way we need it. The lake is the only large source of clean water around. It is the reason everyone gathers here.

Water is life.

I can almost hear the anticipation of our troops, that tense, adrenaline-charged silence as they clench their teeth and hold their positions in the face of the horror hurtling towards them.

'They must only hold them for a while,' I say to Anne. 'Long enough for the Cyclists to feel they've won some sort of victory when our lines begin to fall back.'

I'm only repeating this for my own benefit; everyone knows what to do. I just worry that Rainbow won't be able to bring himself to do it.

'Rainbow will be fine,' she says, rubbing the back of my neck, 'though it goes against everything he believes in to lose. Even if it is strategic.'

I hear her laugh quietly, but cannot detect any humour in the sound. I doubt if anyone will find anything funny for quite some time. That is if any of us are left alive to laugh when all of this is over.

Ever seen the way an ocean swell will rise up and envelop a cliff face?

It slides towards it, then suddenly rears up and smashes itself to smithereens, the water running into every nook and cranny of the rock, winkling out everything loose and sucking it back into the ocean. It is a dramatic sight, sudden and furious and all-encompassing. And there is a sound, a roar of such magnitude that your senses are overwhelmed and you feel as if you too will be sucked back by the water, dragged down and drowned amongst the kelp and the waving arms of long-dead fishermen.

It is this sound which rises up from the desert as the Cyclists finally clash with our front lines: a raging sea of mutation smashing itself against the cliff face of our resolve.

My instructions to Rainbow are clear: Hold them for as long as you can without taking too many casualties, then fall back behind the support lines. Do as much damage to the bikes as possible. Without them they're about as functional as a person without the use of their legs.

He'd sneered at me when I said this. You could hear it in his voice. 'You do pretty damn well without legs, Zac. I've never seen you struggle too hard to get around.'

And he was right, of course. I do extremely well without legs, but that's because I'm used to it.

'You know what I'm getting at,' I snarled back. 'Take out the bikes and you cripple the damn things. They won't adapt as well as I have. They don't have the same support network.'

'Oh, is that what we are, a support network?'

'You know,' I said wearily, 'with the way you twist things, Rainbow, you would have had a great career as a politician or maybe in advertising.'

'What's advertising?'

'Nothing important. Those sorts of things never were. I'm just trying to make a point. If you listen now and don't shoot your mouth off without thinking, you might be around later to reap the rewards.'

'Okay.' There was a sulky tone in his voice, but he did listen. And by listening he would find, I hoped, a way to live through the day.

Weapons favoured by the Cyclists range from knives

and machetes through to lengths of old bicycle chain attached to a leather thong around their wrists. In close, their hand-sharpened teeth can be used to devastating effect. The use of conventional firearms stopped years ago as people ran out of the ammunition needed to feed them. Most of it was used up during the wars which ravaged the planet. Then the remainder disappeared as people formed into tribes and went about marking out their boundaries. You still see the occasional gun, but they are nothing more than ornaments, symbols of a world that no longer exists.

As for our people, we use some bows (up until today these were only ever used for hunting), knives, clubs and spears.

The two groups are fairly evenly matched in weaponry, but we, I feel, have the added advantage of cunning and experience. Over the years, the Originals and I have had more combat experience than probably all of the Cyclists combined.

We have had to survive enemies far more devious and well equipped than mutant ex-health freaks on bicycles. Try avoiding the American secret service or hand-to-hand combat with giant scorpions if you really want to know what trouble means.

The Cyclists always attack in a V formation, the front riders ready to sacrifice themselves to provide an advantage for those that follow. The result of this is that their attack strikes at one point, then spreads to either side, moving further and further away from the initial contact. But because they keep coming from behind that first contact point as well as working off to either side, they will eventually break through and spread around behind the defending troops, forming an X shape. The two side sections then perform scissor movements, catching defenders between the two lines and snuffing them out of existence.

This is the reason we have Rainbow and a contingent of his most fearless Offspring as a roving band behind the front line. As soon as they see exactly where the Cyclists' arrowhead intends to strike, that is where they will take up their position. No matter what, they are to stop the riders breaking through the line and spreading out behind it to perform their scissor movement.

We seem to be succeeding.

Rainbow's people hold firm, like I'd hoped, the Cyclists breaking against them. After that massive noise of them meeting, the sound fell back to something akin to a pub brawl. Most of the sound, though, came from the Cyclists. I'd instructed our troops to remain as silent as possible through all of the encounters, to not give vent to the rage and desperation they felt.

Not until we're ready, that is. And then they can let everything out.

According to Anne, the bikes are piling up, the broken figures of Cyclists draped across them, while the troops that follow try more and more desperate manoeuvres to either get over the top or around the fallen.

They are taking huge casualties, but then so is Rainbow.

'Don't you think it's long enough?' Anne asks. 'They're still holding, but is it worth the losses? If Rainbow falls back now they'll follow for sure.'

I tell her to give the signal, and the next second my

ears are assaulted by the sound of Anne blowing through an old cow horn for all she's worth. It is a harsh noise, but mournful at the same time, and it cuts cleanly through the clutter of battle sounds.

Then everything stops. Just for a second there is a pause of perfect silence, deep and empty, as if the desert had tired of our violent scratching and simply opened up and swallowed everything.

I could be completely alone here for all I know, adrift in a granite boat on a sea of shifting sand.

Then that weird cry of the Cyclists rings out again, but louder this time, filled with victory and promise. I can picture their skull-like faces grinning in triumph, the thought of endless water and food pictured in their minds, as they rise up on the seats of their bikes, massive legs and buttocks beginning to pump with renewed energy as they prepare to surge forward, their arms swinging chains and machetes victoriously around their heads.

And fleeing in front of them are Rainbow and the Offspring, carrying their wounded and dead. I can picture them strung out in a ragged line, moving back from the screaming Cyclists under the cover of our archers, looking like an army in complete disarray.

The reason I wanted the Offspring to be our first line of defence, rather than the Originals or even the natural humans among us, is a simple one. As strangely deformed as they are, the Cyclists still see themselves as human, while the Offspring, who look far more human than they do, are considered to be 'creatures'. The newly old versus the truly new.

That's why they feel comfortable eating them.

The Offspring consider being killed or captured by the Cyclists as the most hideous fate that could befall any of them, and will do anything at all to avoid it (a perfectly understandable attitude, all things considered). For that reason alone, they make the finest front-line troops anyone could hope for.

'The Cyclists are regrouping,' Anne whispers. 'They'll be charging soon, before the Offspring make it back past the second line. They want to catch as many out in the open as possible.'

'They're good tactics,' I say, grinning in the general direction of her voice. 'If I was them I'd probably do the same thing.'

I can feel her eyes staring at me, the heat of her speculation.

'No, you wouldn't,' she finally says. 'You don't think in short-term goals. You're always looking past them, looking for something that will last.'

'I don't look at anything at all,' I reply, still grinning. 'Except what's been stored away from when I could.'

'That's not what I meant. I wasn't suggesting . . .'

I hate it when people make what they think are accidental slips in language around me. And then feel they have to somehow go back and re-say what they meant in a more politically correct way. Just because I can neither walk nor see, it doesn't mean that I no longer use words associated with those actions, or don't allow those around me to use them.

'Don't worry about it, Anne. Just give the next signal the second they charge.'

The desert is hot and dry and flat. It looks as hard and permanent as anything on earth. But the truth of the matter is nothing like that.

It is like termite-infested wood.

The surface looks solid but, underneath, it is honeycombed with small caves, streams and caverns, which spread out from below the lake in all directions. It was from these subterranean passageways that the Originals and I first emerged to try and find ourselves a decent place to live.

Our knowledge of these places gives us something of an advantage and, once we were aware of the Cyclists' intention to take over the lake and destroy us in the process, we began working on a plan which relies as much on what we can achieve underground as it does on what we appear to be doing on the surface.

There is a particular channel which leads from the lake and goes off in a north-westerly direction. I have never seen this waterway, but the Originals and the Offspring know it well. It is one of the areas where they hunt.

What is special about this channel is that it is broad and flat and lies relatively close to the surface. Ever since the Cyclists began to gather in force, Slap and a large crew of his people have been working around the clock to create a lethal surprise, something that ought to take the wind out of the Cyclists' attack for quite some time.

The Cyclists have always been difficult, so self-obsessed and self-righteous that any attempt to appeal to something outside their limited range of vision has always met with disaster. We did not want them as enemies; it was they who created the present situation.

In our early years at the lake, when the only Cyclists we saw were in small groups, we attempted to make some form of truce with them, but that was about as successful as trying to hand feed hyenas.

In our final attempt, Rainbow's father, one of the Originals, went out alone with a written message and a basket of fresh salamander. The next morning we found the basket, still filled with our offering, on the outskirts of our camp. His hand, still clutching the message, was lying on top.

Rainbow has never been quite the same since. None of us has.

With a roar like a flash flood barrelling down a normally dry watercourse, the regrouped Cyclists charge after Rainbow's fleeing troops. There is so much pent-up rage in the sound it is a wonder the retreating Offspring don't simply freeze in their tracks. It certainly scares the hell out of me, and obviously pulls Anne up short as well because there is no sound from her cow horn.

'Anne!' I shout, and her name comes out all high and squeaky, as if I was a kid again calling out to Mum in the middle of the night after an especially bad nightmare. Except this nightmare is very real and very dangerous, and if Anne doesn't react in time we're all dead.

I hear her gasp once, as if I'd just woken her, then an intake of breath and the sound of the horn calling out across the desert. That sound will not only alert those on the ground in front of us, but also the two Originals who are underground at the spot where we dammed the watercourse.

While the Originals and Offspring were working down there, they closed off most of the exit from the lake to the watercourse, leaving only a trickle running through. Then they went to work on the roof of the channel, thinning it down until only a skin remained at the surface, enough for people to walk across, but only just.

At the sound of Anne's signal, the two Originals remove the chocks holding the mini dam in place, allowing the water to rush along its natural course once more, but with the entire pressure of the lake behind it. Hopefully, the two who are down there to set off the trap will be able to surf the rush of water downstream until they can reach a deeper cavern then swim back to the lake. They say they will be able to do this, but I have the distinct feeling they are sacrificing themselves for the overall good of the group. I know Slap spent a lot of time with them last night and it sounded like they were saying their goodbyes.

What happens next shocks even me, and I am the one who planned it all.

There is a rumble, which is more physical that aural, as if a giant has taken the earth and given it a damn good shake to make it come to its senses. The rumble increases to a roar which drowns out the sound of the charging Cyclists. This is followed by a series of loud thumps, each hard on the heels of the one before it.

It is the thin skin of hard-packed desert sand collapsing along a large section of the watercourse, literally disappearing before the charging Cyclists' eyes.

Then the screaming starts, high-pitched and horrible, the sound of creatures who know their time has come.

The way Anne describes it, it is as if someone slashed at the desert with a massive plough, opening up a furrow over a hundred metres in length, a living furrow, one which boils with all the fury we are feeling. The unleashed water from the lake tears along it, and the Cyclists, at full tilt in pursuit of the Offspring, are unable to stop. They pour into the gap in the desert like lemmings, shrieking as they plunge into a torrent which sucks them down into the bowels of the earth, drowning them in the very element they are so eager to possess.

It will carry them down into the caverns and lakes under the surface where their bones will be picked clean by salamanders and scorpions, joining those of the Americans who followed us there all those years ago.

'My God, Zac,' Anne says, her voice faint at the power we have unleashed, 'what have we done?'

'What we had to,' I reply.

From the plain below I can hear shouts of triumph as the Offspring turn back on those few Cyclists who made it across the trap before it was sprung. It is gratifying, even though I know it will be short-lived. We may have stopped the Cyclists for the moment, but they will regroup, and we have to be prepared for the next phase of their attack.

The counterattack comes much sooner than expected.

Ever since our apparent victory I've been trying to get information about what is happening back at the lake with Slap and whatever is causing that huge cloud of dust from the south-east. There is a lot of confusion and many conflicting reports coming from that area, but the one thing everyone seems to agree on is that a force at least the size of that in the desert is approaching.

There does not, however, appear to have been an engagement of any kind.

Slap has ordered his troops as best he can around the lake, but he too is unsure about how to proceed. They have sighted gangs of Cyclists along the edges of the cloud, but it seems as if they are as confused as everyone else.

At times it appears as if they are attacking whatever is coming our way, but that simply doesn't make sense. There are other reports which state that the Cyclists appear to be celebrating, almost leading the cloud along. Any scouts Slap sends in that direction are either being intercepted by the Cyclists or, if they manage to avoid them, being absorbed by whatever is in that cloud.

I need to be down there to get a better notion of

what is happening, but to leave my post on the boulders would be premature. There is much to be done to cement our advantage in the desert.

Victory—even a small one like ours—can cause incredibly stupid behaviour. And of all the stupidity which comes just after we unleashed our water trap, mine is probably the worst.

You see, I stop paying attention. Not for long, but long enough for disaster to reach its long, hooked claws in our direction and tear out a few throats.

All around us on the boulders there's a-whoopin' and a-hollerin' going on, and I'm enjoying it. Against what appeared to be overwhelming odds at the start of the day, we have come at least part way triumphantly. It is cause for celebration and selfish of me to try and stop it, all things considered. The cheer that goes up when Rainbow climbs the boulders to give his report is amazing . . . and, I might add, deserved. He has managed to overcome his natural desire to stand and face the Cyclists, to never give a single millimetre to them, and retreated to victory.

He is a hero, a great one, and our applause is heart-felt, my voice as loud with praise as all the others.

I can smell him standing in front of me, hear his laboured breathing, but it is some time before he speaks.

'You were right,' he says, and the words came out as if through clenched teeth. It hurts him way down in his soul to admit it, and I admire him even more for being able to stand here and do something I know he hates.

'It wouldn't have worked without you there,' I reply. 'You were the key. If you hadn't turned and run like I asked, no-one else would have. I imagine we'd all be dead now if it wasn't for you.'

'Hardly,' he whispers, 'but thanks for saying so.'

And then we both burst into relieved laughter.

The Cyclists hit us from the front, as if they've ridden clean through the flash flood we'd created to stop them. A large contingent must have already been making their way around the base of the boulders even before the trap was sprung, somehow blending in with the landscape. The suddenness of the attack is such that we are almost overwhelmed before we even know what is happening.

The only hint we have is the hissing of their tyres as they come up the track which leads from the plain. There are no warnings from our sentries; the Cyclists having taken care of them on the way up.

I feel Rainbow's hands on my shoulders, and for a brief second think he is about to embrace me, then I topple over backwards, hitting the ground so hard the breath leaves my body completely.

And while I struggle to get some air back inside me, the air around fills with the cries of the Cyclists and the screams of the wounded and dying.

Anne's voice rings out over all the chaos, 'Get to Zac and Rainbow, get around them . . .' And as I roll around in the dust, gasping like a fish out of water, I feel a bike tyre roll onto my outstretched arm, pinning it to the ground. There is a banshee-like scream from just above my head and I feel the distinct whistle of a machete blade whiz past my ear.

It strikes something and hot liquid sprays against my cheek.

Oh, God, I think, I've been hit so hard I can't even feel it. Then the pressure of the tyre on my arm eases and falls away, and I hear, as well as feel, the thump of the Cyclist hitting the ground next to me. Another heavy weight falls across the lower half of my body.

'Anne!' I scream. 'Fall back to the lake. Don't worry about me. Get to Slap and regroup. You have to defend the lake. Rainbow! Rainbow!' But in all the noise I know that no-one will hear me.

I lie on the ground and wait for the kiss of another machete.

Though I've adapted well to my handicaps, there are times when they suddenly seem to gang up against me. This is definitely one of them. I feel more helpless than I have in years, unable to get into any position which will allow me to roll the weight off my lower body and sit up so that I can get a handle on what is happening.

No-one is calling my name any more, and all I can hear are the laboured grunts of those struggling all around me. It's frustrating and frightening, but if I start calling out it will probably only alert one of the Cyclists to my predicament. And if I do happen to get the attention of one of my people, it will just distract them from the Cyclists, and to do that is generally fatal.

Instead, I lie as still as possible, trying to work out the progress of the battle.

I know that Anne and her people will handle the situation effectively. Not only are they fresh and unaffected by the encounter down on the plain, but all of them are well versed in martial arts, Anne having been trained since birth by her parents who had run a karate school in Melbourne. At the very least they'll be able to hold the Cyclists off long enough to escape back towards the lake. I'm more worried about Rainbow and the few Offspring who followed him up the boulders. They are at the point of exhaustion from their previous battle and hardly ready to handle a raiding party of suicidal Cyclists.

Dust, the smell of blood and the stench of Cyclists fill my nostrils, creating a picture of absolute confusion. I've had about enough of playing possum and listening to the violent struggle taking place, so I ease myself up on my elbows and feel around for the body which has me pinned down. It is across my waist and the stumps of my legs and, when I push against it, I realise it is one of our own. Whoever it is had taken the blow the Cyclist meant for me, and paid the ultimate price.

With an enormous effort I manage to push it away enough for me to sit up. I have a pretty good idea of where to head and start to knuckle my way along, staying as low to the ground as possible (which is relatively easy when your legs end just above where your knees should be). It is like trying to wade through rough, shallow water which swirls and tugs you in several directions at once. Bodies and bikes knock me this way and that, but I manage to stay upright and heading towards the path back to the lake. That's where Anne will be making her stand, ensuring the Cyclists pay dearly for any advances they have made.

When I hear Anne call out my name, I think I've actually made it to safety, but I can't be more wrong. I've made my way straight into the semicircle of Cyclists surrounding her. Her shout is a warning rather than encouragement. All I hear, however, is her voice and, once I have it pinpointed, I move even faster towards it.

There is the sudden, loud hiss of bike tyres from behind and an astonishingly strong skeletal arm wraps itself around my neck and lifts me off the ground, holding me helpless and suffocating in its grip.

I scream, but no air escapes my throat.

Bucking and struggling for all I'm worth, I try to loosen the Cyclist's grip. It is like trying to make an impression on a tempered steel bar. Nothing seems to have any effect on the arm around my neck.

'Zac! Zac!' I can hear Anne still shouting somewhere off to my right, but her voice seems to be fading and my ears are filling with a rush like water draining from a bath, everything dissolving into a long, slow gurgle which increases in volume as the sounds of the battle move further away. Images begin to swim through my mind: Edie running in front of me as Marvin and I wheel our way along in pursuit; Violet and Mauve leaping from the swamp, their eyes ablaze with murder; light falling through the open hatch of a water tanker; Aboriginal drawings flickering around the walls of a cave, brought to life by torches; children singing and dancing on a wide sand floor; fungus which glows with its own internal luminescence; my chest covered with the sleeping wrigglers; the sun so bright it burns my eyesight away in welcome.

No mutant bike rider is ever going to take my memories from me.

Using what strength I have left in my body, I swing the stumps of my legs upwards and reach behind me as far as I can. My fingers scrabble for purchase against the Cyclist's plastic helmet and, for a brief second, I think they might slip off, dropping me back with such force that my neck will simply snap from my own weight. Then I find some purchase at the back of the helmet, my fingers catching and sliding underneath. I dig them in as hard as I can.

The Cyclist screams so violently next to my ear I think I'm going to end up deaf as well, but it never eases the pressure on my throat. With the very last skerrick of strength I have left, I swing my lower body downwards, pulling as hard on the helmet as I can.

I feel a sickening ripping sensation through my fingertips, then we go down in a tumble of dust and blood. Air rushes painfully down my windpipe and into my lungs. As they fill I feel myself swelling with an almighty rage, as if I am possessed by something much larger and angrier than myself. It seems as though there are several Cyclists trying to crawl over me at once. I lash wildly, striking at everything with whatever I hold in my hands.

A voice I know is screaming 'Ediiie! Ediiie!', and it takes some time for me to realise it is mine—about the same amount of time it takes me to work out that there are no longer any Cyclists crawling all over me.

In fact, apart from my breathing, there is total silence. I swing around, my ears searching for trouble, but everything is still.

'Christ,' a voice whispers from close by, 'he tore the top half of its head off with his bare hands and beat the damn thing to death with it.'

'Zac,' Anne says quietly, 'we've stopped them for the time being. Put that thing down. We're going to have to fall back to the lake. It's all right, the Cyclists have gone now.'

I feel the tension in my body dissipate and let the heavy helmet fall from my numb fingers as friendly hands grab my arms and lift me from the ground. I can't work out why I'd been calling Edie's name when I'd been battling the Cyclist. It has been years since I've even mentioned her or Marvin out loud. All I can think is that in my moment of panic I'd called out to the one person who means everything to me, even though she is dead.

The trip back down to the lake is confusing. I am still groggy from my fight with the Cyclist and rather disorientated and, if Anne wasn't running along next to me with her hand on my arm, I'd probably think I've been captured.

But as we get closer and closer to the lake, the welcome smell of water brings reality back and I relax knowing that we are approaching a degree of safety.

'I've given orders for everyone to fall back to the lake, Zac,' Anne says over the sounds of our retreat. 'I'm pretty sure the Cyclists that attacked were only a scouting party that got through our troops early on. There was no-one to back them up, and after their initial surprise we finished them off quickly. I thought you were gone, though.'

'What happened?' I ask.

'You tore its helmet off, taking most of its scalp with it. The thing just went nuts. It basically thrashed itself to death—with a little help from you.'

'Where's Rainbow?'

Anne is suddenly silent.

'Anne?' I try again. 'Where's Rainbow?'

'He's dead, Zac,' she replies quietly. 'When they first hit us he stood over you. He wasn't carrying any weapons. He got between you and a machete. I'm sorry. There was nothing any of us could do. The two of you were cut off for a couple of minutes.'

I feel tears forming in my dead eyes and don't hear anything else she says. Rainbow and I had always had our differences, but that doesn't mean I can't feel pain at his passing, doesn't mean I love him any less. Even the welcome smell of the lake fades as grief floods my emotions.

'Rainbow,' I whisper, 'swim deep, my friend. The water welcomes you.'

I hope that is where Rainbow has gone, to the water. It is one of the stories we tell the children, that death is nothing but an endless waterway filled with the most succulent foods and populated by everyone who has ever cared for you.

Hopefully, it will be where I meet Edie and Marvin once more.

14

It is late afternoon by the time we make it back to Endsville, our town built around, on and under the lake.

The troops following behind us have been holding back constant incursions by the Cyclists, who appear to have taken our desert water trap in their stride. Their losses, which must have been many, do not appear to have slowed them down as much as I'd hoped, and they pursue us with the dedication of sharks following a blood trail through the water.

They can scent victory, and it drives them to make bolder and bolder attacks on our rearguard.

What we first thought of as an army of a few hundred is obviously much larger. Either that or they're receiving reinforcements from those approaching from the south-east, which is a problem I'm now going to have to concentrate on. It's hard enough containing the Cyclists we're already aware of without having to contend with an even greater number who haven't even engaged in battle yet. They'll be fresh and eager to join the fray, which does not bode well for our tired troops.

I know I have to concentrate, but all I can think about is Rainbow and the sacrifice he made.

'What's our plan of attack, Zac?' Anne wheezes as she

jogs along beside me. I can smell the dust, sweat and blood of fallen Cyclists radiating from her body. 'Attack?'

In the state I'm in, the word sounds foreign. It takes a few seconds before it seems to compute in my brain. 'I don't think we'll be doing much of that any more. For the time being we'll just have to rely on our defences. See if we can just tire them out.'

'What?' Anne's anger flares quickly, even through her obvious exhaustion. 'You've always said that attack is the best form of defence. Just because you blame yourself for Rainbow, it doesn't mean the rest of us have to suffer because of it. You'd better start thinking, Zac, while you still have something to think with, otherwise your head will be stuck on the front of someone's handlebars and most of the others who rely on you will find themselves as bikie bouillabaisse.'

'Leave me alone,' I mutter darkly.

'Don't you do this!' she snarls. 'I've seen you get depressed before, and this is not the time or place for it. We can't just sit around and wait for you to sort your head out. *Lives depend on you!* My life. Slap's. Everyone's. You think Rainbow stood in front of that machete so you could get depressed and leave the rest of his people to be murdered? Well, do you? DO YOU, ZAC?'

Memories flit through my mind like bats at night, dark shadows that sometimes seem to have form, then simply dissolve away into nothing. I feel like someone has drained the essence from my heart, leaving only an emptiness behind. I don't care a hoot for what Anne is saying, even though every sensible part of me knows she is correct. Images of Marvin burned to a crisp in the swamp fire and Edie dried away to skin and bone out on the Nullarbor assault me, ripping at the soft edges of my sanity.

'People are always sacrificing themselves for me,' I finally say, the words sighing from my throat. 'They're always dying.'

'You self-righteous, self-pitying, self-indulgent idiot!' Anne spits from between clenched teeth. Then she slaps me so hard it throws off balance the two Offspring who are carrying me. The three of us hit the dirt in a tangle of arms and curses.

The Offspring are up off the ground immediately, throwing themselves at Anne. No-one . . . and I really mean no-one . . . ever hits Zac, the great Googlymoogly, the one who took the Originals through the darkness into light.

The altercation has brought our little convoy to a sudden halt and I can hear people running to Anne's aid and others getting ready to support the Offspring. All of a sudden it sounds as if we'll be facing civil war as well as the threat from the Cyclists. And it occurs to me that once again it is my fault. Anne is right, I am being self-indulgent, and it makes me angry at myself.

'STOP!' I bellow from my undignified seat in the dust. 'We can't fight amongst ourselves. It will only help the Cyclists. Let her go. What she said is right.'

'She struck you,' someone says from close by.

'And it's done me a power of good,' I reply. 'Will you please help me up. It's time we were moving. There's a lot to be done, and if we don't hurry it'll be too late.'

Strong arms lift me from the ground once again. As we begin moving, I catch another whiff of Endsville, a combination of cooking fires, water and many bodies who have been living close together.

It is the smell of life . . . of the future.

'Good to have you back with us,' Anne says from beside me.

'Thanks,' I reply. 'Thanks for everything. There's nothing like a good slap in the chops to get your mind back on track. I'll try to keep the depression down to a minimum.'

'I'm sorry I hit you.'

I chuckle. 'No, you're not. You're just sorry you had to.'

When the Originals and I first erupted from the waters of the lake, Endsville did not exist. There was just water and sand and scrub, and a few dozen refugees living in humpies around the shoreline.

Over the years more people arrived and we built houses on the edges of the lake, wooden houses with rooms and windows (okay, they don't have glass in them, but they're windows all the same). The Originals and the refugees worked together, scavenging materials from the one or two deserted farmhouses in the area, making do with stuff that any decent builder would have rejected.

And when the houses were finished, they started on the lodge in the middle of the lake. It is an amazing structure, secured by poles and ropes to the bottom of the lake, and big enough to house most of the Originals, who have never particularly liked to sleep too far away from water. The lodge is the focal point of Endsville, the source of our strength. In some ways it is a symbol of what the Originals represent, a cross-over between land and water, reverse evolution.

In time, Originals and humans began to interbreed, which resulted in the Offspring, who are the perfect balance between the two races: probably exactly what Edie's parents wanted to create when they first crossed fish and human genes. All it took was a couple of stages of evolution to achieve the desired result.

The Offspring prefer to live in floating houses, little more than rafts really, which dot the surface of the lake, drifting this way and that depending on the whims of the breeze.

It is a picture book image, tranquillity itself, and it is my task to try and preserve it for the future.

Expectation is what I feel as we enter the town. What I hear is virtual silence.

The old folk and children who gather around our party as we make our way through the houses to the edge of the lake are tense, waiting for word of what will happen.

When we left late last night to take up our positions, it was generally thought that our return would be triumphant, the flash flood our trump card which would defeat the Cyclists. This is not the case. Even though we have experienced a victory, it is not definite enough to hold the enemy back, and the townsfolk know they are close on our tails.

What they want from me are words of comfort, something that will make them feel that their futures and those of their children will be secure. I can offer nothing of the sort. In fact it takes all my effort to stop myself screaming, 'Run for the hills. Save yourselves.'

Unfortunately, there are no hills, except for the one we've just retreated from, and to save themselves they need me.

I can remember a saying from before: Life's a bitch and then you die. Apart from the fact that it's pretty damn sexist, it's also very apt for our situation. Everyone's recent lives have been hard and brutal, and if I don't do something about our present situation, they're going to be short as well.

Eventually we stop and I can tell from the gentle lapping of water that we're right on the edge of the lake. The two Offspring set me gently on the ground and step back. Everyone is waiting for me to say something, but I feel at a loss for words. There is nothing truthful I can say which will give them hope.

The silence stretches on endlessly as I try to find the right words.

Eventually, a hand touches me lightly on the shoulder, causing me to jump.

'Zac, it's me, Slap. Anne told me about Rainbow. I'm sorry. The waters will be kind to him. We'll see that he dives deep.'

'Take him out to the lodge,' I say quietly. 'I want to spend some time with him before you take him down.'

'Of course,' he replies. There is a pause while he waits for me to add something, but I'm still lost in a whirlwind of possibilities, none of them good.

'Zac,' he says finally, 'what do you want us to do? We're trapped between them now. We have to work out our defences.'

'Of course,' I finally reply, though I'm not exactly sure of what I mean by that. 'I guess you'd better start ferrying everyone out to the lodge. We can plan better once we know everyone is at least safe for a while.'

Slap starts barking orders and there is a sudden flurry of movement all around as people rush to take whatever they think is precious. It's going to be very crowded out on the lodge, but at least it will keep us safe from the Cyclists for a while. One thing we know for sure is that they can't swim, but they're very adaptable, so who knows how long that safety will last.

'Come on, Zac.' Anne's comforting voice comes from

right next to me, and I gather she's been there ever since we'd got back to Endsville. I'd lost track of her after we'd settled our differences. 'Let's get you out to the lodge and start getting everything in order.'

As we start out across the water I feel the beginnings of a breeze from the south-east. It brings with it a faint odour of dust and close-packed bodies, and I know I'm smelling the army approaching from that direction. There must be thousands of them for their scent to carry this far.

'Big cloud build-up coming,' one of the Offspring on the raft mentions to no-one in particular. 'Looks like a storm front.'

This is good news as far as I'm concerned. A storm will make the waters of the lake impassable for anyone except Offspring and Originals, which will definitely work to our advantage. It will also make life around the shoreline extremely difficult for the waiting Cyclists.

Rain is something we rarely get out here, but when we do it makes up for all the time it was absent, falling in sheets so thick it is impossible to see for more than a metre or so in front of you, whipping the lake into a seething froth that the Originals and Offspring can only negotiate from under the surface.

The lodge, though, is far enough above the reach of the waves for everyone to remain safe and relatively comfortable.

As we cross towards it I sit quietly, holding Rainbow's dead hand and thinking back to happier times, back when it was just myself and the wrigglers and our problems were, by comparison, smaller in number and easier to cope with.

15

By the time we have everyone ferried out to the lodge, the mood at the lake is as close to mass depression as you can get, thick and heavy like the moisture-filled air from the approaching storm. Every now and then lightning crackles and thunder rolls ominously off to the south. We've never attempted to gather all of Endsville on the lodge before, and the situation is exceptionally crowded. Even with the Originals and Offspring staying mostly in the water, there are enough humans among us to make it pretty desperate.

I've had Slap recall all of his people from the south-east. There's no point putting up a defence there now. There are too many coming from that direction and, since we're still unsure of who's inside the dust cloud, I think it's safer just to leave well enough alone.

We are under siege; there's no other way to describe it.

Mind you, it's not a bad place to be besieged in, since it offers guaranteed escape routes for Offspring and Originals, and it provides a constant source of food and water for the rest of us. But even though we can probably survive here forever if we can keep the Cyclists away, it will hardly be an existence. We'd have to spend the rest of our lives trapped on a wooden platform surrounded by water. And I don't even want to consider what will happen if a fire starts out here.

Not even an hour after the last rafts leave the shoreline, the Cyclists start arriving, riding in long, orderly lines, their shrieking and screaming drifting across the water like celebrations from hell itself.

They crowd the north-west shore of the lake in their hundreds, almost as if our flash flood has done them no damage at all. It won't be long now, I think, before they start wiping out all the hard work that has gone into creating our town.

'Bastards!' Anne says viciously from beside me.

'Mutant bastards!' I add, in a weak attempt at humour.

'They're going to burn it all down, aren't they?'

'Probably. But they're only houses. We can rebuild them.'

'If we ever get back to shore again.' Anne's voice has a sense of loss to it, as if she's already seen our future and it's bleak. 'You'd better come back inside, Zac. They've laid Rainbow out and they're waiting for you to say the words.'

'There aren't any words for what I feel,' I mutter. But I know it is my task to conduct the last rites for someone as honoured as Rainbow, sad as it might be. 'I'm getting sick of saying goodbye.'

'It's your duty,' is all she says.

The mood is sombre when Anne and I enter the main part of the lodge. There is the smell of torches and the rustle of many bodies packed closely together. No-one speaks, only the occasional cough or subdued sob breaks the silence of the crowd.

Anne takes me to the Entrance, a large opening in

the very centre of the lodge which leads into the lake. Below it is the way into the tunnels and, when I have finished my eulogy for Rainbow, Slap and one of the senior Offspring will swim his body down to where a hole leads far into the bowels of the earth, so far that no-one has ever plumbed its depths.

The Originals and Offspring say it leads to eternal water, where everything that has ever swum swims on forever. I don't know if they're right, no-one does. But I guess it's as good a place to end up as any.

Rainbow will be happy there.

I have prepared nothing, my mind too caught up in the problems of Endsville and the two approaching armies for me to compose words. But as I stand alongside Rainbow's body, the entire population of this town in the middle of nowhere gathered about me, they spill from me like rain at the end of summer.

'Back when the Originals and I first emerged from the tunnels and joined the others who were already here, Rainbow had not been born. Endsville has been his entire life, and he has given that life to protect it. He never knew what the world was like before, the same as many of you now here. Everything he knew was derived from our experiences. But he learnt that what we have here is worth protecting. We called this place Endsville because it was, to us, the end of all our journeys, the end of running and being afraid. AND WE MUST NOT BE AFRAID! Rainbow was not afraid when he stood in front of the Cyclists. If just for a second he thought that we'd cower and whimper in front of these things, he would have laughed at you. Yes, it's sad that he is leaving us, sad that we won't have him with us to tell stories and boast and argue. But he *is* gone, and we must honour his memory by staying here, protecting what was his as well as ours.

This is the future we have here; the past is there along the shores of the lake, bloodthirsty and blind to anything but its own greed. We must never give this up, never back away from those things we believe in.'

I stop briefly to catch my breath. I've said much more than I anticipated. Outside I can hear the rumble of thunder mixed with the growing cacophony from the Cyclists as they loot the houses along the shoreline. It is hard to tell the two apart at times.

I lean forward and place my hands on Rainbow. 'Go now, my friend, swim deep with those who love you. I'll see you there.' Then I push gently and feel his body topple away from me. There is a splash, followed by two more as the others enter the water to guide him down.

I hear the fearsome crackle of lightning striking the surface of the lake, followed by the first rain shower.

It is as if the sky itself is weeping for him.

Normally we would spend the night telling stories of Rainbow, laughing and crying over his memory, but there is too much to be done.

While those of us who can't operate easily in the water go about shoring up every opening into the lodge except for the Entrance, small groups of Originals and Offspring cruise around the shoreline just under the surface of the water trying to work out what the Cyclists' next move will be. As I see it, we're at something of a stalemate. We can sit out here in the lodge pretty much forever, while they hold the shore. Since they can't swim and bicycles don't float, there doesn't seem to be any way they can get out to us. Any attempt at building rafts or even a bridge will be bound to fail because we'll be able to destroy anything like that from under water.

I've given Slap instructions to try and capture one of the Cyclists to see if we can winkle some sort of information from it, but since they seem to speak such a bastardised form of English the chances of us learning anything are slim. But we have to try, our options are getting fewer by the moment.

All around me there is the sound of hammering and sawing as we rip apart every fitting and piece of furniture in the lodge to act as barricades across windows and doorways, while the Entrance boils with the comings and goings of the Originals and Offspring. Reports they bring back are not encouraging.

The Cyclists are tearing through Endsville like the plague through medieval Europe. Many of the houses are already aflame, the roar and crackle mixing with the sounds of the storm. The light rain is not enough to douse the fierce conflagration, fuelled by wood so dry it literally explodes when touched by fire. Lightning and thunder sizzle and roll around us and the air seems charged with electricity, though I can't decide if this is the fault of the storm or the general atmosphere inside the lodge. Even our wounded are up and lending a hand, everyone moving with such a frantic sense of urgency that it leaves me feeling useless. The only assistance I can lend is that of my brain, which is so battered by everything that is going on it doesn't seem to want to function properly. I feel like beating my head against the wall in an attempt to get it working again.

There is something wrong—apart from all the catastrophe around us—and I can't seem to put a finger on what it is. The Cyclists must have known that we would retreat out into the lake, and that from here we are pretty much impregnable. It doesn't seem right that they have allowed us to get back here so easily. Sure, they suffered dreadful losses when we unleashed the flash flood, but after that they almost seemed content to let us retreat at our own pace, only providing a minimal amount of harassment to keep us moving.

The thing about the Cyclists is that they never leave anything behind. Total destruction seems to be their driving force. So why, I keep asking myself, have they let us get out here? What else do they have up their sleeves?

We work feverishly all night and, as morning approaches, I begin to hear something which stands out from all the other sounds. It is like a long drawn-out groan which rises in intensity, then ends with a sudden, loud shout . . . Ahhhhhhhhhhh HUP! Ahhhhhhhhhhh HUP! It is a long way off, but over the last few minutes it seems to have got closer.

'What is it, Anne?' I ask when she is next to me.

'What's what?' She is distracted, like all of us.

'That sound off in the distance, the groaning or chanting or whatever it is?'

'I can't hear anything, except for Endsville being burnt to the ground.'

'Listen.'

And she does, but she still can't isolate that sound from all the others.

'Maybe it's from the group in the south-east,' she says. 'Slap reckons they'll be here by morning, so maybe it's coming from them.'

I listen for a while. 'No, it's not from that direction. It's coming from somewhere behind the Cyclists, I think. Back in the direction they first attacked.'

'Your hearing is better than mine, Zac. I can't get a handle on it at all, but I'll tell some of the Offspring patrolling the shoreline. Maybe they can work it out.'

'Do that,' I say. 'It may be important.'

'Everything's important right now,' she mutters, walking away from me.

There is a sudden, loud commotion from the direction of the Entrance, wild thrashings and screaming coming from the water. I think they have found a way to swim, because mixed into the chaos is the very clear sound of a Cyclist.

The sound of wet footsteps approaches and I tense, not exactly sure of what is going on.

'Got one,' Slap says happily from right in front of me. 'Silly bugger thought it could take a drink from our lake. The moment it stuck its head down for a slurp, I pulled it straight under. It's a bit waterlogged, but alive. What do you want to do with it?'

'Bring it here,' I reply grimly. 'I'd like a little chat.'

I can't believe the fact that it's laughing at me. Here it is in the middle of enemy territory, held captive by the very things it wants to destroy, and every time I ask it about that sound I can hear it breaks into a long, hideous cackle, it's vile spittle spraying across my face.

'Want me to hurt it?' Slap asks.

'No,' I reply without hesitation, 'that would make us as bad as they are.'

'It killed Rainbow. I've got every right to hurt it.'

'No, Slap, it didn't kill Rainbow, *they* did,' I say, pointing as best I can towards the shoreline. 'You can't blame just one of them, or take it out on just one either. Torturing an individual might make you feel better, but it won't do any good overall, will it?'

I can feel him glaring at me, but he knows I'm right. No matter how bad your situation, if you can't stick by principles, there's hardly any point existing at all.

The Cyclist has been silent during Slap's and my brief altercation, but soon after we stop arguing it suddenly starts to rave. It vomits words at me. Basically they're all just gibberish, but every now and then I pick up some word or phrase I still recognise as having begun as English.

'What's it saying?' Anne asks after it has stopped raving.

'I'm not sure. I can't understand most of it, but it keeps repeating a phrase. Something about "the big thing" or "bringing the big thing", that's all I can make out.'

'You reckon that's the sound you've been hearing?'

'Maybe,' I reply. 'But I tell you something, whatever this big thing is, it's got to be what they think will get them out onto the lake. Maybe they've got a boat or something, an old pontoon they think will ferry them out here.'

'A boat's not going to help them, we'll just tip it over or set it on fire,' Slap interjects. 'It is physically impossible for Cyclists to beat us on the water.'

'What if it was a metal boat, one of those big landing craft they used in invasions?' Anne asks him.

'We'd find a way.' Slap's voice contains a tinge of uncertainty, but he still sounds confident enough to do what he says. And I tend to agree with him, anything on or under the water won't be able to compete with Originals and Offspring.

'There's no point sitting here and arguing amongst ourselves until we really know what this big thing is,' I finally say. 'Until then, I want everyone to continue what they're doing. When it's light we'll have a better idea of what we're up against.'

Slap stomps off to resume command of the teams harassing the Cyclists along the water's edge.

'You want me to take this thing out and kill it?' Anne asks, referring to the captured Cyclist.

I'm tempted, even after what I said to Slap, but can't bring myself to order someone's death, even if it is barely human. 'No, hang onto it. Tie it up somewhere and bind its mouth; I'm getting ill smelling its breath. It may come in handy, as a hostage or something.'

'You've got to be joking. You think they'd care about a hostage?' she says, her voice registering disgust.

'Not really, but you never can tell.'

I hear Anne moving away and barking orders. She's not happy with me, but there's nothing I can do about that right now.

Outside the rain has stopped. I can smell the burning houses along the shore and still hear the screams and shouts of the Cyclists. That odd sound is closer as well, and I'm sure the others on the lodge can hear it by now. With morning so close, it won't be long until we know what it is.

If it's a boat, especially a metal one, we're dead.

16

It's not the metal boat I feared. It's much worse.

For the last couple of hours we've been hearing the arrival of the second army from the south-east, but they've camped on the section of the lake furthest from us. This group is huge, from all accounts, but it appears to be keeping itself separate from the Cyclists. They are too far from us to make out as individuals, all anyone can see is a seething mass of figures, mostly obscured by smoke from the smouldering town. Seething is the operative word; their numbers seem to reach into the thousands. But as yet they have made no attack or serious incursion into our territory.

As dawn finally makes itself known, Anne and I are standing at one of the three windows we haven't yet boarded up. Though the storm has pretty much blown itself out during the night, there are still squalls coming through, so I imagine the surface of the lake is covered in small whitecaps. Not a huge amount of rain has fallen, the storm having comprised of mostly wind and electrical discharges, so there is still a strong smell of burning coming from the remains of Endsville.

Apart from that strange chant, the Cyclists have fallen silent, their joy at having entered and razed our town having blown itself out during the night with the storm. None of them are sleeping, though. Anne says they are all lined up along the edges of the lake staring out at the lodge. Their silence is almost more terrifying than their screaming.

'They're waiting for something,' she whispers, though there is no need for quiet.

Ever since she's been able to make things out on the shore, a long double line of Cyclists has been edging its way closer and closer to the lake. They are arranged on either side of a massive rope, though what they're towing is still hidden by the pillars of smoke from the burnt-out houses.

'Can you see it yet?' I inquire, knowing that my question is pointless, the second she can see 'the big thing' she'll let me know.

'Sort of,' she mutters. 'I can just make out a shape through the smoke, but it's still . . .' Anne's voice fades away.

'What? What is it?' I continue. 'Can you tell if it's a boat?'

I hear the Cyclists chanting, 'Ahhhhhhhhhhhh HUP! Ahhhhhhhhhhhh HUP!' But it is now huge, the only sound our enemy is making.

'For Christ's sake, Anne, what is it?'

I hear her gasp once, a small intake of breath, but it is enough for me to realise that whatever she's seen is more than she wants to comprehend.

'IS IT A BOAT?' I finally shout.

'No,' she replies, her voice so small and weak I almost want to reach out and comfort her, but there's not time for that. 'It's an old petrol tanker. One of those things they used to deliver fuel to service stations. There's no truck on the front of it, just the back bit with the tank.'

'Where the hell did they get that from?' I'm in awe that anything like that would still be around.

'I don't know, Zac,' she continues, 'but from the number of Cyclists needed to pull it, it's got to be full.'

And suddenly the implications are clear to me.

'They're going to set the lake on fire, aren't they?' Anne asks rhetorically. 'We're all going to die.'

'Not without a damn good fight,' I reply.

It's odd, I think, how at one stage I tried to destroy the Originals with fire myself, yet ended up being their salvation. Now it looks like I'm going to suffer the fate I once intended for them. I guess that's what is called poetic justice.

It takes the Cyclists most of the morning to manoeuvre the massive petrol tanker across the sand and down to the water's edge. It sits there, half in half out of the water, squat and ugly and caked with rust. According to Anne, the Cyclists seem to be having trouble opening the valve to release the fuel and are attempting to smash it off with axes and clubs, their shouts of frustration ringing out across the lake.

The delay in our destruction is appreciated, but it will only be a matter of time before fuel spills out over the surface.

'Maybe the fires in Endsville will set off the fumes the moment they open it,' Anne says hopefully. 'It might blow them all to kingdom come.'

'Yeah,' I add, 'and pigs may fly and come swooping down from the sky to rescue us.'

'Hey!' she snaps back. 'We live and breed with people who can breathe under water, who's to say there aren't pigs flying all over the world by this stage. They used to be able to do all sorts of stuff with genetic engineering.'

I laugh. 'Somehow I don't think flying pigs were on

the American military's agenda, but I take your point. How's everyone taking the news?'

'As badly as you'd expect if you just found out you were about to be char grilled. There are a lot of goodbyes being said.'

'Maybe you should go and make a few of your own,' I add, sadness filling my voice.

'Nah,' she says softly, her arm going around my shoulders, 'I haven't actually given up hope yet.'

'Always the optimist.'

Since the petrol tanker's arrival, Originals and Offspring have been preparing to head back down to the caves and tunnels under the lake. From there they should be able to make it to another place of safety, but once again they'll be underground nomads for who knows how long. It is not something any of them thought they'd have to do again.

As for us humans, though, there is nowhere to go. The trip back down to the underground system is simply too hazardous to attempt. But we're accepting of our position. And most of us are too old now to pack up and leave, to take on new lives and adventures. That is something for the young.

Somehow, those of us who remain will make sure that the Cyclists pay dearly for destroying our lives and sending our loved ones into exile. Though exactly how we're going to do that I'm not yet sure. Something will come to me, though. It usually does.

It happens quickly and with much violence.

Anne, Slap and I have been sitting around trying to plan some kind of counterattack which will take the attention of the Cyclists away from the petrol tanker. We even contemplated trying to blow the thing up ourselves before they'd released any fuel, but doing that will spray burning fuel everywhere, including across the lake. The lodge would go and there would be few survivors, so it would have a similar effect to what the Cyclists are already planning.

We'd pretty much decided to attempt to haul the tanker into the lake and sink it out of reach of the Cyclists. There would have to be a fairly major diversion for this to work, and it would take virtually all the Originals and Offspring to drag the thing into the water, but it was the best we could come up with.

I'm about to start giving orders when there's an incredible roar of noise from the shore.

Everyone panics.

The only thing I can think of is that they've released the fuel, but I can't get a word of sense out of anyone. Neither Slap nor Anne is close by, both having taken off to their respective positions the moment the alarm was raised.

It sounds like battle, but no-one from our side has given any orders to attack, so I can only guess at what's happening.

'SOMEONE TALK TO ME!' I shout, and right then I'm grabbed under both arms and hauled away.

'They've got canoes,' a voice says. 'Get ready to defend the lodge.'

And I hear the sound of Originals and Offspring diving into the lake.

The next second I'm put down and hear Anne. She's close by, excited, shouting orders, then she turns to me.

'It's the other group, the one's from the other side. They're attacking the Cyclists.'

'What?' I can't believe what I'm hearing. 'Are you sure?'

'You should see it,' she says breathlessly. 'A group of them came from the direction of the granite boulders they must have been circling around. And there are hundreds more crossing the lake in canoes. They're not coming anywhere near us, just heading for Endsville.'

'Who are they?'

She's silent for a few seconds, and it's almost as if I can hear her mind working.

'People,' she finally says. 'Real people, like you and me. They've got the Cyclists surrounded, driving them down to the edge of the water.'

In their panic, the Cyclists are doing extraordinary things, some of them leaping their bikes through the air and landing on the arriving canoes, swamping them in the shallows, the shoreline boiling with the struggles of those in the water. Others are still all over the petrol tanker, trying to force open the valve.

'Where's Slap?' I ask.

'Getting ready to attack, of course,' an elated Anne exclaims.

'Attack who?'

'The Cyclists, of course. These are people, Zac; they've come to help.'

'How do you know they won't turn on us the second they've finished with the Cyclists?' I ask. 'Anyone with any sense will take out the stronger enemy, then finish off the weaker one later. Come on, Anne, use your head. They're just here for the water, like the Cyclists.'

'They're *people!*' she says, and I can hear the desperation in her voice. She wants to believe, doesn't want me ruining the only hope she has, but I have to bring her back to reality.

Sometimes I hate being in charge, it makes you do things that hurt individuals because you have to think of the greater good, the good of the whole group.

'Tell him,' I say, my voice firm and unflinching, 'he's got to hold back, keep our people fresh in case they turn on us. I'd like to believe they're here for us just as much as you do, Anne, but I have to be sure. If we help them and they turn on us, where will we be then?'

She storms off without replying, but I know she'll do what I ask. No matter what, Anne's a soldier first and foremost and will follow orders, no matter how much it might hurt her to do so.

I sit at the window, my head resting against the frame, and listen to the sound of the battle coming across the lake.

It rages all afternoon.

Slap eventually comes and sits by me. He's the only one. All the others are too transfixed by the battle across the lake, their hopes rising and falling as it wages this way and that.

'You want to tell me what's going on?' I finally ask after he's been sitting there quietly for an hour or so.

'I didn't think you knew I was here,' he says quietly.

'It had to be you, Slap. You'll be sitting there when I die. How's Anne?'

He laughs. 'Oh, she's on one of the rafts tied to the lodge, along with pretty much everyone else. She's sulking. She literally spat your orders at me. I thought she was going to hit me at one stage, she's so upset.'

'And what do you think? Am I right?'

'It's a good strategy,' he finally answers, and I know from the way he says it that he disagrees. He wants to be out there fighting alongside the people, pulling Cyclists to their doom under the lake.

I decide to change the subject. To have the two people I respect most disagreeing with me makes me more than a little uncomfortable. Perhaps I'm wrong and the ones who are now attacking the Cyclists might decide to turn on us simply because we didn't help them. That's the thing about people, you never really can tell how they'll react to anything.

'Describe it to me,' I ask him, 'I need to get a picture of what's going on.'

He talks in a monotone, completely without emotion, which for Slap is an indication of just how angry he is.

'The Cyclists are completely surrounded. The group which came from the boulders seems to be a holding force, cutting off the Cyclists' avenues of escape. They split into two streams, coming on either side, then joining with the ones in the canoes. The Cyclists are trapped around the tanker, but they're holding out fairly well. I don't think they'll last all that long, though, there are just too many of the others.'

'Can you see who's leading them?'

'No, it's too chaotic. Must be someone in the canoes. That seems to be where their main force is concentrated.'

I was puzzled. Even though the Cyclists had managed to find an old petrol tanker somewhere out in the desert, I couldn't work out where anyone would get a flotilla of canoes. Then something occurred to me, something from way back when I lived with Marvin and my parents and we had a swamp at the end of our street. The swamp where this whole saga with Edie started.

'Can you see what the canoes are made of?'

'It's hard to tell, but it looks like metal of some kind, though that can't be right, can it? Canoes are made from fibreglass or wood, aren't they?'

'Or corrugated iron,' I add. 'They're making them out of roofing sheets. You can do it if you seal them properly, fill in all the nail holes and stuff.'

Slap sounds confused. 'How do you know this sort of thing? I didn't think you were a canoeing kind of guy.'

I laugh. 'Used to be. Once. A long, long time ago.'

18

It ends at sunset.

The remaining Cyclists have had to leave their bikes and are clustered on top of the tanker. According to Slap there can only be a couple of dozen left, all the fight knocked out of them. They sit up on the metal tank, their heads bowed with exhaustion as the victorious army stands around, their triumphant cries reaching easily across the water.

As the sun falls, their camp fires ring the lake on all sides.

'What now?' Anne asks.

She's returned from watching the battle and sits at the window with Slap and me, all of us nervous now that the battle has ended.

'We wait.' It's all I can think of. 'And make sure the Originals and Offspring are ready to leave. There's too many of them to hold off.'

'And what about the rest of you?' Slap is uncomfortable about leaving us behind, though I know he'll do it if he has to.

'We'll surrender,' I reply. 'Maybe they'll show mercy, since we're human.'

'Can't we just send someone out to talk to them?' It's

Anne, always hopeful.

'I'll think about it. If nothing has changed by morning, I'll do it. There's no way anyone else is going to end up like Rainbow's father.'

It's enough of a reminder that peaceful intentions aren't always met with a peaceful response.

'Post sentries and everyone try and get some sleep.'

No-one does, of course, least of all myself. I lie listening to harried pacing and whispered voices, the sounds of people worried about their futures. I wish there was something I could say to ease their fears, but my mind has emptied of everything positive it ever had to offer. I feel drained, exhausted and depressed.

Sometimes I can hear singing from the shoreline as the triumphant army celebrates its victory.

The question is, will they be celebrating again tomorrow?

19

The tiny raft rocks precariously on the surface of the lake as we head out towards the waiting boat.

'How many are there on it, Anne,' I whisper, knowing how far voices carry across water.

'Six, I think.'

'What are they doing?'

'Just watching us. They've got an anchor out, so they're just sitting there waiting.'

I feel underneath my shirt for the knife I've got hidden away. If things go badly out there, I want to make sure I take one or two of them along with me. And maybe I can give Anne enough time to escape. I'm pretty sure there are a few Originals swimming underneath the raft who will help her get away. Even though I've strictly forbidden anyone accompanying us, I know Slap will find it impossible to restrain himself. He forgets how well I can hear, and I'm sure I heard bodies slip into the water as Anne and I left the Lodge.

The boat had appeared at first light, paddled out about half way between the shore and the lodge. It was a real boat, too, an old Halvorsen without a motor. We'd sat around and waited for them to do something, but they, in turn, did exactly the same. I was sick of waiting, so I had a raft prepared so that I could confront them. I'd wanted to do it alone, but wouldn't have known where I was heading, so Anne talked herself aboard. I wasn't happy about it, but she wouldn't take no for an answer.

'Hooly dooly,' she suddenly exclaims.

'What?' I'm instantly alert, ready for trouble, even though there was no sound of alarm in Anne's voice.

'You should see the spunk sitting at the front of their boat. Talk about gorgeous. He can invade my territory any time he likes.'

'*What? Are you nuts?*' I can't believe she's talking like this. 'We're just about to try and negotiate the survival of our people and you're drooling over some male who could have us killed the second we get there.'

'Oh stop it,' she says. 'Just because he could kill us doesn't make him any less attractive. They stopped the Cyclists and haven't attacked us, so I'm not so sure they want to kill anyone right at the moment. Stop being such a bore. Anyway, there's a real ugly one with him as well, so it's a nice balance.'

I'm literally spluttering with fury when she adds, 'Now be quiet, Zac, we're nearly there.'

I can feel Anne back-paddling the raft, slowing us down as we approach the waiting boat, her technique sure and confident after years of practice.

There is a gentle bump as we touch, and then the impact of feet landing on the raft. It shifts under the new weight. Then there is just silence.

I can feel eyes boring into me, but I just sit there. If anyone is going to say the first word it will have to be them; they're on our territory after all.

And we wait, no-one moving or speaking. It seems to go on endlessly. I can sense Anne's nervousness from beside me.

Finally, a voice comes from the boat.

'Have you got any idea how long Edie and I have been looking for you, Zac?'

Familiarity charges through me like electricity. I cannot believe what I am hearing, who I am hearing. Tears spring to my eyes and I reach out my hands imploringly.

'Marvin?' I say, my voice little more than a squeak. 'Edie?'

Our raft is rocked again as I feel others jump aboard it, then the touch of a hand I never thought I would feel again. My emotions are going haywire and I keep thinking that I must be dreaming, this couldn't possibly be happening. But the hand touching me is warm and full of life.

I raise my own hand and run it across a face which is obviously scarred, and there are these odd bumps under the skin which I know are pieces of jewellery sealed there long ago in a fire.

'Edie?' I say again.

'How are you doing, Halftrack,' the voice I've been hearing in my dreams for fifteen years says gently, 'long time no see.'

'Don't tell me that spunk on the boat's your brother,' Anne says in a whisper from right beside me. 'He doesn't look the least bit like you.'

Dawn. I can hear it coming to life all around me.

Marvin, Edie and I sit at the same spot on the boulders where I lost Rainbow, which seems like a lifetime away but is really only a few days.

We have been talking all day and night in the lodge, only making our way here when we could sense the morning lurking down below the horizon. There is so much we have told each other, so much more to tell.

But we have been silent for some time now, giving the day time to wake. It is pleasant sitting here and listening to the first calling of the birds and the occasional scurries of rabbits through the rocks. For the first time in years I can listen to these sounds for what they are, rather than trying to read something threatening into each of them.

I am at peace, content with everything.

Marvin, according to Edie, has grown to be much like I was before the car accident, tall and strong. He has a quiet way about him, though I think that hides a mind which is resourceful and very focused. He has crossed a great deal of country in extremely trying circumstances after all, and he seems to have the respect of everyone who followed him.

Edie is still Edie. Though I know she bears hideous scars from the fire in the swamp which also disfigured myself, nothing much has changed about her. She is still light-hearted and sees the positive in most things. Hopefully we'll be able to start again where we left off. We'll be the ugliest couple on the face of the earth, but since neither of us cares a damn about appearances I can't see that making a difference either way.

I'm just too happy to care what anyone else thinks.

'It's beautiful here,' Edie says quietly. It is still strange to hear her voice.

'Beautiful?' To me, it seems a surprising thing to say. 'It's just sand and rocks, but if you think it's beautiful I'm not going to disagree with you.'

'But it's so green,' Marvin adds. 'As far as I can see, Zac.'

'Must have been the rains,' I say. 'I've always known the desert could change quickly, but I've never seen it.'

'I'll always be able to tell you what things look like, Zac,' Edie says, her hand resting along my forearm.

There is finally true peace in Endsville. The remaining Cyclists have been contained in an enclosure constructed from the ruins of the town, but when we get back from here I'm going to set them free. They're no longer a threat. In time and with patience, there may even be a place for them among the rest of us. They certainly have skills we don't possess, skills we can all benefit from if we work together.

To tell the truth, we're all pretty sick of fighting. The lake is big enough to support everyone, if we take things carefully. And since we all exist, as Marvin and Edie put it last night, we may as well try and work out a way to exist together.

There will be disagreements, naturally, as pretty much everyone has a grief they want to lay off onto someone else. But that puts us all in the same boat, doesn't it? We will confront things as they come, work it out in a way that doesn't leave anyone with a grudge. The trick is to make sure we don't repeat the mistakes that brought the world to what it is today.

In the meantime we will begin the rebuilding of Endsville, but even that will change. There are so many more of us now, so many different types of people, and people who aren't quite people, that it will be a new place altogether. And I guess it really isn't an end any more, but rather something that is just beginning. Perhaps we will rename it, call it something a bit more positive. I'm actually tempted to call it Rainbow's End, in honour of my friend, but we'll all have to agree on that.

I will sleep soon, so that I can listen to Marvin and

Edie tell me more of their story with fresh ears.

There are so many years to catch up on, it may take years to tell. I want to know how they found each other, how they survived when so many others didn't, and how they came to bring so many people with them.

And how on earth they worked out where to find me.

As far as everyone about and under the lake knew, we were pretty much the end of everything. Funny how you can be so wrong sometimes.

But there will be plenty of time for stories tomorrow. We have all the time in the world.